Old Dogs and New Tricks

Argentina Ryder

Contessina Publishing

Contents

Chapter 1

"There he is."

Jessica Cruz strolled into Nadine's Salon, pushed past the flustered girl at the front counter and walked straight toward Nolan Reynolds and his stylist's chair. "Where have you been?" she asked, one hand on her hip. She pointed at her hair and ignored the astonished looks from the other patrons. "Look at this mess! Look at it."

Nolan finished sweeping up around his chair and tried not to snicker as she advanced on him. "Oh, dear." It really was that bad. The older woman's tresses resembled a shredded party wig. Nolan had many questions. "I'm sorry I wasn't here for you. But even the wicked need their rest, you know that, Jess." After setting the broom down, he reached out and hugged her. "What happened? Who did this to you?" Nolan touched a strand of dry hair and frowned. "I hope you didn't pay for this."

"No. It was my granddaughter." Jessica groaned and collapsed into the chair. "She got some idea in her head to style me up for a family portrait—you being unavailable and all," she said, her mouth turned into a pout. "Well, I hope your vacation was worth it." Then she smiled, at ease now that she was in the salon chair. "I need to know all about your trip. Did you have a good time?"

"Absolutely. You'll be the first to hear all the juicy details." Nolan ran his hands through her hair and stared at her reflection in the wide mirror at his stylist's station. Yes, it was salvageable, but barely. "What do you think about trying a stacked bob? We can keep some of these layers and it will give you a lot of movement." Nolan pulled some strands and worked out how much hair he had to work with —her granddaughter had gone to town with the scissors. "It'll be a little shorter than we usually do your hair, but we need to get rid of all these shredded ends. You'll see a lot more volume back here, too. I'll make it super cute."

"Whatever you think, dear." Jessica's eyes closed as Nolan made his plans. "You're in charge here."

An hour later, the older woman beamed at him and peeked at her reflection as she presented her credit card to the receptionist. "Nolan, darling, you're a miracle worker." She grinned and pressed some bills into his hand as a gratuity. "I'm glad you had a good time on your trip," she added before she exited the salon.

"Another satisfied client." Angel, the front desk receptionist, applauded as she approached Nolan's workstation. "I live in constant admiration, watching you work your magic on these harpies. Ms. Cruz scares the shit out of me."

Nolan snorted as he tidied up. Those older women were his bread and butter here at this salon, and not that hard to keep happy. "She's a pussycat who just needs someone to listen to her problems and agree with everything she says." He swept all her hair clippings into a small, neat pile. Now where was that dustpan? "Have you seen my—"

Angel picked up the dustpan hidden away under his station, and handed it to him, attentive as always. "You know, I never asked you about your trip. How was Cozumel?" Angel had bright pink streaks in her long black hair and had manned the front desk at Nadine's for the last two years. Her mother owned the fashionable salon, nestled in the quirky, gay-friendly Montrose district of Houston, for twenty years. "Was it fun?

Nolan had worked at the salon for the last four years yet managed to grow a sizeable client list among Nadine's picky patrons with his innovative stylist skills and entertaining stories from the gay side of the tracks. "Cozumel was wonderful. I hung out on the beach and caught up on a trashy book that I wanted to finish."

Angel sighed. "I'm super jealous. You look like you caught some sun, all tanned and shit."

He took a quick glance at himself in the mirror. She was right—his skin glowed with a golden tint that set off his gray eyes quite nicely. He'd styled his own dark brown hair loose today, soft curls that brushed his shoulders and added to the relaxed vacation vibe.

After admiring his reflection, he turned back to Angel, who held up the trash can for him. "Did you meet anyone interesting?" she asked as he discarded the clippings.

Nolan shook his head, but not in disappointment. "Wasn't that kind of trip. I just needed some 'me time,' you know?"

The phone rang. Angel nodded and beamed at Nolan, then raced back to the front desk to answer it. He wiped down his station and prepared for the next customer.

By the end of the day, Nolan had repeated the details of his trip so many times he'd memorized a quick version of the story. It had rained when he departed Houston last Wednesday, but the sun shone the entire four days he was down there, perfect weather for relaxing on a beach. No, he didn't go with anyone, but that was by design. He needed some time to clear his head and rest, especially after the car accident last month, when his roommate Diego's car had been hit as they headed home one night from their favorite dance club.

Nolan didn't like people knowing he was still rattled by it.

No, he wasn't sure what was going to happen with Diego's court case, but he would meet the lawyer handling things tomorrow morning. No, Diego had done nothing wrong, but the woman that hit them was suing for damages and refused to drop the case.

No, he hadn't talked to Jake the Snake, his ex-boyfriend who'd broken his heart, and had no plans to get back together with him.

Nolan was doing fine on his own.

His stomach growled when he clocked out for the day, so he stopped by Ping's on the way home and picked up some beef with broccoli. Diego's car, a blue Honda CRV, was in its space when he pulled his old Volkswagen Passat into their apartment's parking area. "I thought you were working tonight," Nolan called out as he stepped inside their apartment and dropped his keys off in the bowl by the front door. "I'd have gotten you some dinner if I had known you were home."

Diego Duarte poked his head out of the bathroom, shirtless with his favorite torn up jeans, and displaying colorful tattoos all over his arms and chest. "That's okay. I'm on my way out. We've got a gig tonight." A tattoo artist by trade, Diego also played bass guitar in Steel Horse, a rock band, and they played some local clubs a couple of times a month. "I fed the boys their supper, and they did their thing outside."

"Thanks." After Nolan set the bag down on the kitchen counter, he walked over to what would have been the apartment's dining room. An extra-long baby gate cordoned off most of the area, and inside, two medium-sized dog crates sat on thick brown blankets that covered the carpet. Next to the crates was a basket of dog toys and two small but excitable pit bull puppies who wagged their tails and yapped as he approached.

All the stress and worries of the day lifted from Nolan's shoulders as he stepped over the baby gate and sat down. "Hey guys. How are you doing? How was your day?" Each dog took their turn, climbed onto his lap, and lifted their faces up for kisses. Their wide, flat heads butted against him as he scratched their wriggling bodies. "Oh, that sounds nice. I had a good day as well, and thanks for asking."

For as long as Nolan could recall, his family had dogs in their homes; always at least one or two spoiled family pets. As he and his twin brother Noah grew older and became more independent, their mom went into dog rescue as a diversion, and now the entire family took part in the activity. Dani Reynolds, Nolan's mother, helped transport dogs from shelters to out-of-state rescues and fostered dogs at her home. Noah ran the rescue's official website and social media accounts. Nolan enjoyed fostering a dog or two for them when he could, and right now, Smokey and Bandit were their guests for the next month, until they found their forever family. "I'm gonna go have some dinner now, but I'll be back later."

After he washed his hands, Nolan waved good-bye to Diego, and sat down to eat his dinner before it got cold. While he ate, he opened up his laptop and navigated to a bookmarked page—'Careers in General Business Administration'—and reread the university's admission requirements, even though he'd looked at the page so often he had memorized the information.

Did Nolan need a university degree to open his own salon? Probably not, if he had the money and the support to back him up those first couple years until he was more established. But when Nolan was twenty, he dropped out of college after a year and a half. He'd always wanted to go back and finish. "Maybe this is the year," he said, and glanced over the requirements and tuition information one more time.

When Nolan didn't get the assistant manager's job at the salon, Nadine told him it was because Joi had been there longer, and maybe that was true. But not having any real business schooling on his resume pricked at his pride, and the missed career opportunity had contributed to that funk that everyone else attributed to his break-up with Jake.

Maybe this was the year to do something about it.

Maybe this was the year.

Chapter 2

The clock on Harrison Crawford's desk read a quarter after five when he finished up a last-minute email and shut down his computer. It hadn't been a court day, and he'd spent all afternoon with Alicia, his paralegal, evaluating notes from last week's case. "I guess you're glad that Mrs. Costa won't be stopping by the office anymore," he said when she entered his office and dropped two thick files on top of his large mahogany desk.

Alicia snorted, rolling her dark eyes. "As much as I hate we lost the case—yes, I'm not sorry that she'll spend some time locked up, even if it's at a minimum-security prison. She was a dreadful woman who never said a friendly word to anyone here in this office, including you, Mr. Crawford. All that work you put in, and not one single 'Thank you'."

Harrison didn't disagree. "I accepted the case as a favor to her husband, but I don't think he realized the extent of her embezzlement." Darlene Costa had taken thousands of dollars from the private school where she worked and spent it on clothes and vacations. He had dutifully represented her as best as he could, but the evidence was overwhelming, and in the end, she pled to a lesser charge. "At least it's over." But now there were new folders, fresh cases to prep. Why not get started tonight?

Alicia shook her head as he reached for the files, her box braids brushing her shoulders. "Not today, sir. Go home and enjoy your evening. You've been working too hard lately."

She was right. Coming in early, staying late—Harrison had spent more time than necessary in his office in the last six months, and Alicia, as well as his law partners, knew why. His house was just too big, too empty for one man. Troy, his son, graduated from college last year and moved into his own place. Not long after, his wife—his ex-wife—Jenny left him for her tennis coach. Why did he even keep the place at all? Some days, it was simpler to stay at the office, where he could be useful. Where he had a purpose, and where people looked up to him with admiration.

At home, all Harrison had were his thoughts.

Later that evening, as he pulled into the long, circular driveway of his Piney Point home, the garage door opened on cue and the automatic lights flipped on, illumining his exquisitely landscaped front yard.

Harrison smiled; he had always been proud of this house —seven thousand square feet on half an acre in one of Houston's most desirable neighborhoods. It was a far cry from the crowded Kansas City apartment he'd grown up in with his mother and older sister. A magnificent stone house with plenty of room for entertaining, though that had been Jenny's arena, and an enormous yard with a pool for Troy and his friends when they were younger.

But now it was just Harrison.

After he changed into a t-shirt and a pair of basketball shorts, Harrison wandered into the kitchen and made himself a sandwich. A bag of chips and a soft drink completed the meal, and as Harrison turned to head back upstairs, he froze. Two items—one package and one thick paper envelope—sat unopened on the kitchen table, and despite his best efforts, he couldn't avoid them much longer.

The package wasn't so bad. An award—heavy and black with gold engraving—from the Harris County Bar Association, noting Harrison as a Distinguished Leader in the Houston legal arena.

The envelope contained his divorce papers.

It had been official for over three weeks, the legal dissolution of his marriage, but somehow, seeing the document made it all real.

Nope. Not tonight. Harrison didn't want to look at either of them right now. Maybe tomorrow. Instead, he headed back upstairs to the media room, his favorite place in this entire house. A few taps on the remote control, and another episode of *The Sopranos* blared out on his big screen entertainment system. Of course, he'd seen it enough times to have whole scenes memorized, but it never got old. When it was time to turn in, Harrison turned the television center off and headed to his bedroom.

He had developed a routine. Harrison would climb into his king-sized bed and reach for the laptop kept next to it. He would open it and navigate to a popular porn site. Why did he still feel guilty, clicking Gay in the category menu? There was no one here to judge him, no one to make sly comments and subtle threats about spilling his secret.

He liked to watch men fuck. He liked to look at their bodies and listen to the sounds they made.

Had Harrison ever acted on these feelings? No. He wasn't doing anything wrong.

He was just looking.

Harrison's finger scrolled along the touchpad until something grabbed his attention—*Muscle daddy barebacks bubble butt twink*.

Yes. Soon, the sound of slapping skin and throaty groans filled the room. Harrison's hand dropped into his boxers and gripped his cock. Three minutes later, he wiped himself off with a tissue, tossing it unceremoniously into the trash can next to the bed before he closed the laptop and turned off the light.

A ceiling fan slowly rotated above him, and he let out a heavy sigh. Harrison would be forty-six this year, and this was his life now.

Chapter 3

Nolan glanced down at the address on his phone one more time, double checking to make sure he wasn't lost. He didn't come to downtown Houston often, and all the buildings looked the same—tall skyscrapers made of steel and glass. But showing up late for his deposition with Diego's lawyer was unthinkable, so he had to find this place soon.

Not the deposition, not yet. That unpleasant experience would take place later. Today, Nolan would meet Diego's lawyer and fill him in on all the details he remembered from the night of the accident. His stomach churned with anxiety just thinking about that night. With any luck, this interview wouldn't take long, and Nolan could head back to work this afternoon to help the gang with spring inventory.

Nolan meandered a few more minutes, but after walking into a Starbucks to ask for directions, he found the right building. Heavy glass doors slid open when he approached, with that frigid cold air that always reminded him of expensive places. He was heading for the eighth floor; Nolan knew that, but still stopped to glance at the large sign in the lobby to double-check.

Law Offices of Barton, Simmons, and Crawford — Suite 801

There was no one else on the elevator. Just Nolan, lost in his thoughts, and when the doors slid open, it startled him. The law office took up the entire floor. Swallowing nervously, Nolan straightened his button-down shirt and pushed his hair back, tucking the longer strands behind his ear as he entered the suite.

A receptionist with a bright smile greeted Nolan and walked him to a private waiting area in the back. "There's an espresso machine on that table, and some bottles of water in the little fridge underneath," she told him.

He muttered a soft "Thanks," and had just fixed a cup of coffee when he heard his name. "That's me," Nolan said and glanced up.

Diego's lawyer looked like what a fancy lawyer should look like. Neat, dark hair, with more than a little silver at the temples. A serious expression but sparkling blue eyes that radiated curiosity when he extended his hand. A good, firm shake as he introduced himself as Harrison Crawford. Not as tall as Nolan, but broader in the chest. His expensive Italian suit had been tailored to fit those wide shoulders, or perhaps made-to-order, Nolan mused, and followed him to his office.

A huge wooden desk with a couple chairs took up one side of the room, flanked by bookcases, but the lawyer walked them over toward a smaller, more casual set-up on the opposite end, next to a floor-to-ceiling glass window, more of a conversation nook with comfortable chairs and tall, potted plants. Some abstract art on the wall caught Nolan's attention. But as Nolan sat down and set his coffee on the table in front of him, he looked up and saw the lawyer staring expectantly at him. "Yes?"

The lawyer chuckled.

Shit, he'd asked a question. "I'm sorry, could you repeat that?" Nolan pushed the nervous butterflies in his stomach down.

The lawyer—Mr. Crawford—smiled. "I just asked if you needed anything before we began. I see you made some coffee."

"No, I'm good." Nolan took a deep breath. "I'm ready."

"Excellent. Well, I am going to explain what we're doing here today, and then we'll talk about the night of the accident." Mr. Crawford outlined the legal process that Diego—and Nolan, by extension—was now a part of. So much legalese, and while Nolan thought he understood what would happen, he appreciated how the lawyer seemed to break things down even more. Nolan understood his role in these proceedings, and why it was so important. "Despite Diego's blood alcohol test proving that he hadn't been drinking and the police report indicating that the other driver hit his car, the plaintiff contends that the accident was because of Diego's reckless driving."

Nolan shook his head. "But that's not what happened—"

Mr. Crawford smiled again. "And that's what we will prove... with your help." His hand reached down and tapped his knee twice before he stood. "I'm going to get my notebook and then we'll talk. There's nothing to be nervous about."

Easier said than done. Nolan didn't believe that, but sure enough, once Mr. Crawford began asking questions, it wasn't that difficult, and Nolan shared everything he recalled from the night of the accident. "I had been moping at the house for a couple weeks," he said in response to the question of why they'd gone out that night. "I was getting over a bad break-up, and Diego was sick of listening to me whine about how all men were creeps and can't be trusted. Anyway, Delirium has a live DJ on Thursday nights, so he thought it would cheer me up."

"Did it?"

"It did, yeah." Nolan laughed and recalled the way his friends supported him when he was down. "I had a great time. Diego had a good time too, but he was just mostly watching over me, I think. Making sure I didn't do anything—or anyone, that I'd regret."

Mr. Crawford nodded and grinned to himself. "He sounds like a great friend."

Nolan nodded. "He's the best."

"Back to that night." Mr. Crawford jotted something down on his notepad. "You said that you two stayed at the club for about three hours, and then walked to his car. How many drinks did you have that evening?"

"Probably... four." Nolan tried to recall each trip he made to the bar. "Not a lot, but enough to help me forget about —" Nolan stopped and bit his lip. "Anyway, I wasn't drunk."

"And Diego?" Mr. Crawford asked quietly.

"Diego doesn't drink. He's been sober for years." At least the entire four years Nolan had known him. "He had a few Diet Cokes, that was all."

"How would you characterize his driving that evening?"

The lawyer crafted his questions carefully so that Nolan could explain as fully as possible, and he appreciated that. "Diego is an excellent driver. The roads were wet because it had been raining, but he always drives slow around Delirium 'cause there's so many people walking to their cars or back to their apartments."

Mr. Crawford's lips curled into an amused smile. "I'm glad to hear he's a safe driver. How was his driving that evening, Mr. Reynolds?"

Just answer the question he asked you. "That evening, Diego drove cautiously. He stopped at all the stop signs and didn't go above the speed limit."

"Good." He wrote something else down. "What do you remember about the collision?"

Nolan frowned. They had gotten to the part of the night where his memories got hazy. "We were talking about a mutual acquaintance, someone who works with me at the salon. He'd brought in a tin of tuna for lunch, but without the paper wrapping, you know? He opened it up and sniffed it and asked me if I thought it was bad."

Mr. Crawford glanced up. "I'm guessing it wasn't tuna."

"It was not. More like Fancy Feast," Nolan said with fake outrage. "Our friend Enrique is not the sharpest tool in the shed, but I think he brought in the cat food on purpose." Mr. Crawford smiled at that, but wasn't writing anything down, and Nolan realized he'd gone off-topic again. "Sorry. Anyway, we were talking about that, and I saw—"

It had happened so fast. "I saw something on my right-hand side. We'd stopped at the stop sign, but then we started moving forward when we got hit. It was red, the car that hit us. I remember seeing the red."

"How did you feel after you were hit?"

That anxiety welled up inside again at the memory. "My head hurt, and I felt sick. Diego got out and looked at the car and—" A fragment of a memory flashed through his thoughts. "He went to see if the other person was okay. Then he got me out of my side."

"You couldn't get out on your own?" Mr. Crawford's brow arched.

Nolan shook his head. "I was stuck. My seatbelt locked, and my head pounded. Everything was spinning."

"Anything else that you remember?"

Nolan shrugged. "I sat on the ground and then—next thing I remember was the emergency room. I stayed a few hours, and my mom came to pick me up and take me back to her house to sleep it off."

"Do you recall any conversation between Diego and the plaintiff?"

"I don't. I'm sorry." By that point, Nolan was unconscious.

"Don't be sorry. Just share what you can to the best of your recollection." The lawyer smiled at him, soft and comforting. "That's all I want from you—the truth."

By the time Nolan was ready to leave, his mind had changed one hundred percent about this experience. Diego was in expert hands. Harrison Crawford knew his shit and had been exceedingly professional, and yet made Nolan feel like they were just talking about the weather or the price of gas.

Even more interesting, Mr. Crawford—Harrison, he told Nolan to call him, hadn't blinked when Nolan mentioned going out because he'd been bummed about his ex-boyfriend, or that they'd spent the evening at a gay bar. Houston, like most urban areas in Texas, was more progressive than other parts of the state, but even so, it surprised him when people—especially older men—didn't give him disapproving, reproachful looks when he spoke openly about his sexuality.

Nolan appreciated that, because frankly, Diego's lawyer was one of those men who only grew more attractive as they grow older. Not that he was old, not by any means; the silver hair sort of aged the man prematurely. As they talked, Nolan put Harrison's age closer to his mid-forties than his early fifties. Some laugh lines on his face, probably from a youth spent outside, and those sparkling blue eyes that just lit up and crinkled each time Harrison smiled.

And those broad shoulders, Nolan's personal kryptonite.

Oh yes. The lawyer was cute.

With any luck, Nolan would look as good when he was this man's age. Harrison's hair was a tad too long on the sides, and Nolan's fingers itched to touch it, to manage those soft curls and style them into submission.

Then, Harrison was staring at him—he'd asked Nolan another question. "Fuck," Nolan murmured to himself. "Apologies. I get lost in my thoughts sometimes, you know, problems with attention—" Nolan touched his temple. "I used to take medicine for it, but I don't like the way it makes me feel."

Harrison nodded. "My son was like that. He took a pill for it." He tilted his head in thought. "I think he still does."

Suddenly, a light switch went off. "You're Troy's dad."

Harrison's face lit up. "I am."

Troy played guitar and sang in Diego's band and was a good friend to both of them. "Now it all makes sense. I wondered how Diego snagged such a fancy downtown lawyer."

"Not that fancy," Harrison said, though his expression suggested he knew that wasn't the truth. "My firm usually deals with more... white collar sorts of crimes. Fraud, embezzling, money laundering. But I jumped at the chance to help Diego out. He's a great kid, and Troy thinks the world of him." Harrison leaned back in his chair and crossed one leg over the other, dropping his notebook on the table. The page was filled with small, neat script, and a few doodles on the edges of the page. "It feels good to work with someone who genuinely needed support. And really, he isn't to blame in this situation. The other party is out to get him because of his past, and I will not let them win."

Diego had a breaking and entering criminal charge on his record from an incident that happened when he was a teenager. From the sound of it, the other party planned on using that to get a fat check out of Diego's insurance, not counting on him to put up much of a defense in court. But Harrison's excitement and indignation about Diego and this lawsuit stirred something in Nolan—and it wasn't just because he was already crushing hard on the older man. "I'm glad you're on our side."

Their eyes locked for a long moment, and Harrison smiled. "Me too, Nolan. Me too."

Chapter 4

Alicia always laughed at the large paper calendar that Harrison kept on his desk. Yes, the shared office calendar on the computer helped organize the firm and kept everyone in the loop, but he preferred the old-fashioned tech that he grew up with, like his desk clock and paper calendar. Harrison enjoyed jotting notes quickly in the edges and glancing down to see a circle in ink drawn around a date, and today, a little note on his calendar reminded him he was meeting his son Troy at their favorite restaurant later for an early dinner to catch up.

For the first time in weeks, Harrison left the office before the end of the workday to beat the rush hour traffic and pulled into DJ's BBQ Joint just after five.

Troy was already there, seated at a table. "Over here," he called out and waved.

Harrison couldn't keep the smile off his face as he joined Troy, smartly dressed in a long sleeve shirt and chinos. Troy had his mother's sharp mind and angular features and Harrison's compassionate spirit, and he loved his son dearly. After the server took their drink orders, he reached out and touched Troy's arm. "Thanks for meeting me tonight. Sometimes I feel like I never see you anymore."

Troy laughed. "Most parents can't wait for their twenty-somethings to move out. But I miss you too, Dad." The server brought their drinks and took their orders. Troy took a sip of his sweet tea and hummed in contentment, but his brow furrowed as he spoke, and his voice dropped. "How are you doing?"

The worry came off Troy in waves, but Harrison shook it off. "I'm good. Busy, but there's nothing wrong with busy. I've got a couple of interesting cases coming up." Once upon a time, Harrison dreamed of his son following in his footsteps, and the two of them opening a law practice together. But Troy's interests went in another direction, and after graduating college, he worked as a sound engineer at the local public radio station, with the end goal of producing music. "How's work?"

They spent a few minutes discussing Troy's new girlfriend, and Steel Horse, the band Troy and Diego started a few years back. "It's going good. We've got some gigs planned for the summer. Might even try to enter a Battle of the Bands at one of the Fourth of July events." Troy's eyes lit up. "That reminds me—thanks again for taking Diego's case. I know you don't usually work with that sort of litigation, but he doesn't have the money to hire a big gun like you."

"I'm hardly a big gun, at least as far as personal injury litigation goes," Harrison answered. "But I think we've got an excellent case together."

Troy agreed. "I hope so. Honestly, I don't know why that lady is going after Diego. He doesn't have any money. Why sue him?"

"I think she's trying to get a payout from the insurance company. She's hoping that they cut her a check, thinking that it's easier than going to court." A smiling waiter brought their dinner orders—two full slabs of ribs and cole slaw. "That reminds me," Harrison said as he spread a napkin over his lap. "I met his roommate yesterday. Nolan Reynolds."

Nolan. Harrison hadn't been able to get the young man off his mind—his bright gray eyes, his crooked smile, or that adorable way he scrunched his nose when he got distracted. He'd been on Harrison's mind all night.

Troy dug into his ribs, and it was a few minutes before he could answer. "I know Nolan. He's a good guy. I'm glad he didn't get seriously hurt in that accident."

"Me too." Harrison poured barbecue sauce over his ribs. "He gave a good account of the night that the accident happened. I think he's the best witness we've got." He looked back up at Troy. "Is he reliable?"

"Nolan? Yeah, he's on the up and up. I met him about four years ago, right when he and Diego moved in together. Nolan had been living with his brother—he's got a twin, right? He and his brother Noah got into a fight one night and Nolan moved out and, after a few days, ended up with Diego. Worked out for the best."

"What did they fight about?" Harrison took a sip from his drink and tried to hide his curiosity over the younger man.

"Nothing huge, just brother stuff, that's what I heard. Noah, the other twin, he's a lot more serious. He got the brains in the family, I guess, and teaches college classes over at the University of Houston, the main campus. But Nolan was always the more popular one, more outgoing, real friendly. I guess he was a party guy at school, but I don't think he finished college. He works over at a hair salon in Montrose." Troy reached for another rib, but paused, holding it up in front of his mouth. "You picked up that he was gay, right?"

Harrison nodded. "He told me. Said they were at a gay club that night."

"Right, right." Troy continued talking as he ate. "Well, Noah's gay too, and I had heard that they fought over some guy and that's why Nolan moved out. But it was a long time ago. He's a good roommate to Diego."

"I'm glad to hear it." Nolan and his friends seemed so open and free about their sexuality. What must it be like to not care about what people thought about you, to not worry about losing your job, your friends, your family?

They ate a few more minutes in silence before Troy spoke again. "Have you talked to Mom recently?"

"I have not." Harrison knew that their divorce hadn't surprised Troy, but it still cast a pall over their conversation. "The paperwork came, making it official."

"She told me." Troy wiped his mouth with a napkin. "She's throwing a birthday party for Bill and wants the band to play. I told her we were busy that night." Troy shrugged. "Is that wrong, to lie about that?"

"Will she pay you for playing?" Harrison reached out and touched his son's hand. "If you don't want to play, then don't. But it sounds like easy money."

"I'm not happy with what she did to you—"

"And I appreciate that. But it's not a reason for you to argue with your mother. It's between us, and frankly, I'm not mad anymore. She was unhappy and found someone that makes her laugh. Good for her." Harrison took a drink from his soda and wondered if he believed that.

"What about you? Are you seeing anyone yet?" Troy asked.

Harrison shook his head. "Not quite ready for that." Troy caught Harrison's eye, and he froze. Did Troy know about his sexuality? Had his ex-wife mentioned anything to their son?

Maybe... maybe it was time for Harrison to share this with Troy, one less secret between them. On the other hand, perhaps it would be better if and when he actually found someone to love, be it a man or a woman. Harrison would tell his son about it then, yes. He wouldn't hide it, wouldn't be ashamed of who he loved.

Harrison would be brave, like Diego and Nolan and those other kids out there who were out and proud.

When the server brought the bill, Troy reached out and took it. "My treat," he said, pulled out his wallet, and handed the check back with some cash.

Harrison's eyes widened. "No, let me pay it."

But Troy shook his head. "Nope. I'm making a decent living now, and I can take my dad out for his favorite ribs once in a while."

Neither of them spoke for a minute, and the pride welled inside Harrison. "Thanks, I appreciate it, Troy."

"No problem." Troy finished his drink and slipped his wallet back into his pocket. "You know, speaking of Nolan —"

Harrison's face felt hot, as if Troy had read his thoughts. "Yes?"

Troy grinned. "I know you said you weren't ready to date, but his mom is a real nice lady. Sweet. Does dog rescue. You'd like her."

Oh. Harrison reached for his drink and quickly took a sip. Was his face turning red?

No, clearly Troy had not been reading his mind because it wasn't Nolan's mother that Harrison was interested in.

God help him—it was Nolan.

Chapter 5

Noah had a Costco membership, so once a month he'd pick Nolan up and they'd go shopping together. Their mom once observed that since they were identical twins, Noah could easily have got a second card for himself and just given it to Nolan to use. But as the brothers grew older, they both realized that these shopping trips were more than just getting groceries. Their lives had diverged, and it was harder and harder to find time to spend together, and shopping was something they both needed to do.

Not that they were identical anymore. Noah kept his dark hair short—too short, in Nolan's professional opinion. Noah also preferred glasses, which gave Nolan, who wore contact lenses, a headache.

Noah had just finished paying for his groceries when Nolan's phone vibrated. It was a text message from Diego. *Got a big favor. Big group just showed up at work and I'm stuck here. Can you meet with the lawyer? He'll be at Delirium in an hour.*

Nolan frowned. Diego was supposed to meet with his lawyer today to discuss the accident and show him the specific route they took that night. But now Diego was super busy at work, which ordinarily was good news. Even with the lawyer giving Diego a break on the fees, this lawsuit was costing him money—money he didn't have. A chance to get some new clients was a great opportunity for Diego.

Will do. On my way.

Nolan held up his phone to his brother so he could read the message. "Can you drop me off at the club?"

"Is it even open yet?" Noah snorted as they headed out of the store. "It's a little early, even for Montrose."

"Probably not, but we're just going over what happened that night. He needs to see where it all happened."

"The scene of the crime," Noah mumbled. Nolan didn't need their twin vibes to tell him the accident had shaken Noah up more than he wanted to admit. "Okay. Yeah, I can drop you off." Pushing the cart to his car, Noah looked down at their groceries. "Want me to take your stuff to my house? You can come pick it up later."

"That would be great." Nolan tossed his arm around Noah's shoulder and squeezed. "This is why you're my favorite brother."

"I'm your only brother, moron." But he reached out and messed with Nolan's hair and laughed.

Twenty minutes later, Noah pulled his Toyota Prius into the empty parking lot of Delirium night club. "I haven't been here in a while," Noah said, looking around. "I think the last time was Pride last year. Hey, is that him over there?" He pointed to a man standing next to a dark blue Mercedes. "That looks like what a lawyer would drive."

It was a sweet car, but it was the man standing next to it that had Nolan's heart beating faster. "Yeah, that's him."

Noah pulled into the parking spot next to where Harrison had parked, and they both stepped out of the Prius. Nolan approached Harrison with a wave. "Hi there. Nice to see you again. This is my brother, Noah." They shook hands as Harrison glanced back and forth between the brothers, silently making comparisons. People had done that to them their whole lives. *I wonder what he thinks about us.* "Mr. Crawford, um, is there any chance that you can drop me off at my place when we're done?" Nolan asked.

Harrison nodded with a bright smile. "Yeah, of course. Thank you for doing this with me today. I'm sorry Diego got caught up at work."

Noah and Nolan hugged, then Nolan waved as his brother drove off. Harrison pulled out his phone and took some photos of the club and parking lot. "Have you ever been over in this part of town?" Nolan asked. Even though the club was closed, Montrose was a vibrant neighborhood during the day, with many popular shops and restaurants all within walking distance, and several large apartment buildings nearby.

But Harrison shook his head. "Not too often." He snapped a few more pictures of the neighborhood, then peered down the street. "Did there used to be a dance club over there?"

Hmmm. There had been a club there, a little before Nolan's time. A leather bar, if he recalled correctly. Now it was a Starbucks. "I think so. It didn't close, just relocated a few blocks south." Harrison turned back to the club, his eyes taking in everything. Even though he dressed professionally, it wasn't an expensive suit and tie like he'd worn the first time they'd met. Today he wore a long-sleeve dress shirt the same shade of bright blue as his eyes, and tight around his wide shoulders. But he'd rolled up his sleeves and the first two buttons of his shirt were open, and it gave him a more casual demeanor that Nolan really liked. "I'm kind of surprised you're doing this yourself. I'd have guessed you had minions to do this for you."

Harrison laughed. "I might have a minion or two back at the office. But in a case like this, I like to go out and see things for myself. And it's nice to get out of the office once in a while, especially on a pretty day like this. Sometimes I feel like I'm stuck up there."

He wasn't wrong; early March in Texas was the best time to be outside. Nolan smiled, that tight, nervous feeling loosening inside him. "Then I'm glad you're getting this field trip. So, tell me what I need to do to help."

"Okay. First, just go through the events of the evening with me. According to Diego, you came here straight from your apartment. No dinner first, no other clubs or places to get a drink. Is that correct?"

Nolan nodded. "Yeah. We weren't planning on staying out long. He just wanted to get me out for a few hours." Had it just been six weeks ago that he'd been so blue? Nolan shrugged. "I was in a funk."

"Break-up problems, right?" Harrison pulled out a small notebook and glanced down at his notes. "When we spoke before, you said that he took you out to get over a break-up."

"Yes. But—" How to explain. "Yeah, I was upset that my ex had cheated on me, but I was mad about a bunch of things. Just—generally feeling like a fuck-up. It's been a rough year, and it's only March." Harrison's eyes widened slightly at the profanity. But before Nolan could apologize, Harrison gave him an empathetic smile.

"I'm sorry to hear that." Harrison closed his notebook. "Can you show me the route you took home?"

"Yeah, of course." They got into Harrison's car, and Nolan held back a gasp. The posh interior was impeccably clean, and the sleek electronic dashboard and soft leather seats casually stated wealth. "This is really sweet."

"Thanks." Harrison started the car, and they pulled out onto the street. "So, you got to the club at nine, stayed a few hours. What time did you leave?"

"Around midnight. I had to work the next day. My salon is over—right there." Nolan pointed down the block as they crossed an intersection and indicated where Nadine's Salon was located. "If you ever need a haircut, stop by. I'm amazing." As soon as the words left Nolan's lips, he shuddered inside. Why did he say that?

But Harrison laughed, those crinkles near his eyes incredibly sexy. Nolan couldn't explain what it was about Harrison that he found so attractive; he hadn't ever dated older men. But something about this man got him hot.

Luckily, Harrison didn't notice. "I might take you up on that. My son tells me I'm due for a make-over."

"That's rude." Nolan laughed, trying to picture this man as Troy's father, but he couldn't. Yes, Harrison was probably closer to his mom's age, but Nolan didn't think of him as someone's 'dad' when they spoke. "I can't imagine why he'd say that. You're great looking."

"Well, I'm just coming out of a divorce, and—" Harrison stopped speaking. Had Nolan said too much? People always told him that his friendly banter came off as flirtatious, even when he didn't mean it. Or maybe Harrison stepped over his own boundaries and into personal territory. "What was the drive like that night?" he asked, as if he wanted to get back to business.

Professional. Right. Keep it professional. "It had been raining. I remember the roads were still wet, that kind of slick shine you see when the headlights hit the pavement." Soon they were at the intersection of the accident. "It was right here."

Harrison pulled over onto the side of the street and stopped the car. "This intersection has a four-way stop."

Nolan nodded, but Harrison wanted an answer. "Yeah—yes. Diego stopped and looked around for pedestrians. There's always people stumbling home at night, and he's very mindful of that. Then we started moving again and—"

Nolan stopped talking. He wasn't sure how long he sat there, silent, but after a moment, Harrison's hand rested on his shoulder. Nolan turned and looked at him and didn't see Diego's lawyer or Troy's father. He saw a handsome older man with beautiful blue eyes and a brilliant smile. "Sorry. I just hadn't thought about it in a while."

Worry lines furrowed in Harrison's brow. "That's fine. Take your time."

Ugly memories of the accident threatened to overtake Nolan's thoughts. He took a deep breath, then slowly let it out. "Okay. We started driving again, and I saw the car coming at us. I guess I thought she was going to stop, but she didn't. It was red, all I saw was red heading toward us. Then I felt the impact against the back of the car." He pointed at the street. "We ended up over here, in front of that Greek restaurant. We faced that way." Another deep breath and Nolan murmured aloud the thought that had spun around his head since that night. "If she'd been driving a little faster, she might have hit me instead of the back of the car."

"Thank God she didn't." Nolan looked up when Harrison said that, and their eyes locked for a moment. "What happened after that?"

"After the car stopped moving—" Nolan's shoulders slumped. "I guess I was in shock. Diego was talking to me, asking if I was okay. He got out of the car right away to see the damage, and to see if the driver of the other car was okay. I was stuck."

"Stuck?" Harrison repeated, even though he knew all of this from their initial interview.

"My seatbelt stuck. Jammed, I guess. Diego had to come get me and, I don't know. He got me out somehow." Nolan pointed to the corner across the street. "I sat down over there, and then the police arrived. I passed out after that." Harrison took some notes again. He looked around at the intersection and all the buildings. "I guess I'm not much help."

"That's not true. You've given me a lot of details, and now I can see what happened more clearly. I think that not only is he not going to lose this case, I believe we have an excellent opportunity for a counterclaim."

"Do you really think so?" Nolan's mind raced at the possibilities. "Diego could really use the money."

"I think we've got a shot." Neither of them spoke for a moment, but the quiet didn't bother Nolan. "Okay then, let me get you back home. How do I get there?" Harrison asked, starting his car. He pulled back into traffic, and Nolan guided Harrison back to his apartment complex, just a couple of miles down the road. "Must be nice, working so close to your home."

"It's great. We lucked into this complex. It's an older building, but an amazing location and we've got some good friends that live here too." Harrison parked and Nolan opened his mouth to offer his thanks for the ride home. But what came out was, "Want to come in for a minute and meet my dogs?"

Harrison's brows reached high into his hairline, and Nolan groaned inside. This wasn't the first time his fucking impulsivity got the better of him. But then Harrison laughed. "Yeah, sure. I'd love to see them."

A hundred worries flashed across Nolan's thoughts. *Was the bathroom a mess? Did we clean our breakfast dishes? Did the apartment smell like puppies?* But it was too late — he had extended the offer and now Harrison was out of the car and following him around the corner to the door of their first-floor apartment.

With a quick prayer, Nolan unlocked the door and stepped inside. A blanket was messily tossed over the sofa and Diego's running shoes were on the floor next to the door. But other than that, everything appeared to be in order. He sighed and opened the door wider as Harrison stepped inside. "Can I get you a bottle of water?" Nolan asked and closed the door behind them.

"Yeah, that would be great." Harrison's eyes darted all over the place in amusement. "Quite the bachelor pad."

"It works for us." Sure, the appliances weren't brand new, and there wasn't a gym like some of the newer complexes. But the rent was affordable, and it had a fenced in area where they could walk the dogs.

Playful barks from the dining room grabbed their attention, and Harrison walked in that direction. "Well, look who we have here."

Nolan grabbed a water bottle from the fridge and set it down on the counter. "The one with the white paws is Smokey, and the other handsome boy is Bandit." He hurried over to them, stepped over the dog gate, and bent down to pet them. His face wrinkled as they licked him. "How are we doing, guys? Need to go pee?"

"Can I help?" Harrison bent down to scratch behind Bandit's ear. The puppy clamored over to meet the stranger and soon both dogs tried to climb him as well. "They are beautiful. How old?"

"Three months." Nolan reached down and picked up one of them, and held the warm, wriggly body close to him. "They'll be put up for adoption in a week or two. They're just hanging out here with us until then, getting socialized and hopefully housebroken."

"That's amazing. Is it hard to say goodbye to them?" Harrison picked up the other puppy and followed Nolan to the sliding glass door. "I don't know if I could do it."

It took a moment to slip the harnesses on the excited puppies, and they headed outside. "It was at first. But now I just remind myself that each dog that I foster has a good family out there waiting for them, and that they're just hanging out with us for a while, chilling with the cool guys."

"A puppy vacation at the bachelor pad." Walking next to Harrison, Nolan laughed as the puppies scrambled around in the grass, chewing on each other's faces and finally finding a spot to pee.

Yeah, he'd miss these guys. "Something like that." There it was again, that comfortable banter. Harrison was still a stranger, and yet Nolan wanted to sit down and listen to all his stories, to learn everything about him. "Thanks again for the ride home."

"It was the least I could do. You gave me a lot of good information, and as the best witness we've got in the case, that made it even more valuable." They headed inside, and Nolan unleashed the puppies and let them run around the apartment. "Which one of them is Burt Reynolds again?" Harrison asked.

Nolan looked up with a confused look on his face. "Who?"

"Their names—Smokey and Bandit. It's from a movie. An old movie. Burt Reynolds and Sally Field." Harrison's expression was priceless—he couldn't believe Nolan didn't know that. "You've never seen it?"

Oof. "I plead the fifth, your honor." Nolan hung his head, dramatically ashamed. "I'm an ignorant child. All my friends say so."

Harrison chuckled. "I don't believe that. But you should watch it sometime. It was a fun movie, as I remember."

"Will do." After Nolan handed Harrison his bottle of water, he pulled out his wallet and fished out a small business card. "And don't forget my offer." He held it up for Harrison between his fingers. "You've got fantastic hair. I'd love to get my hands in it one of these days."

Harrison's eyes widened, but the spark of interest at Nolan's light flirtation was undeniable. Harrison felt it, and Nolan was never wrong about these feelings. "How can I resist an offer like that?" Harrison took the card, their eyes still locked on each other. "Thanks for everything today and tell Diego that I'll be talking to him soon."

The door closed behind Harrison, and Nolan leaned against it, screwing his eyes shut. "What was that? What are you doing?" he asked himself.

One of the dogs barked.

"No, you're right. That wasn't very smart," Nolan murmured.

But no one ever said he was the smart twin.

Chapter 6

The chilly, bright examination room at Harrison's cardiologist's office had several posters affixed to the walls, detailing the human heart and its inner chambers. Dr Singh, his cardiologist, pointed to one of them and chided Harrison about his high cholesterol levels. "I'd cut down on the red meat, maybe eat some more vegetables," he said as Harrison buttoned up his shirt. "But overall things look good."

Give up red meat? The voices inside Harrison's head laughed. *Sure.*

Harrison squinted at the bright afternoon sun as he headed back toward his car. The first two items on today's to-do list went much faster than he'd expected—renewing his driver's license and seeing his doctor. Maybe he hadn't needed to take the whole day off after all. But Harrison still needed to get a haircut, and since he hadn't made an appointment, most likely he'd have to wait a while for Archie, his barber, to work him into his schedule.

You've got fantastic hair. I'd love to get my hands in it one of these days.

Harrison pulled the small business card out of his wallet and stared at it. *Nolan Reynolds, stylist.* Oh, this wasn't a smart move. The kid was cute, but there was no way he'd really be interested in someone like Harrison. Young, handsome, charming—Nolan could have anyone he wanted.

Nolan had just been nice to him because he helped his friend. Yeah, that's all. But—if he was just being polite, then there was nothing wrong with taking him up on his offer to style an old man's hair and let him do his good deed for the day.

Harrison snorted at how easy it was to convince himself. *Why not?*

Traffic was light, and thirty minutes later, Harrison wandered into Nadine's Salon. A young Hispanic girl greeted him. "Do you have an appointment?" she asked, the pink stripes in her hair as bright as her broad smile as she glanced at her computer screen.

Oops. "No, I don't. But I—" Harrison opened his mouth to say that he was friends with Nolan Reynolds, but that wasn't quite right either, was it? *Were they friends?* "Nolan told me to come by for a haircut."

The young woman—Angel, according to her name badge —scanned the monitor. "He doesn't have any more appointments available today, but I can fit you in on—"

"Wait." Nolan appeared behind Angel, who gasped in surprise. "You came." Nolan, like all the other stylists, wore all black—a tight-fitting t-shirt tucked into dark jeans. For someone as outgoing and gregarious as Nolan, the dark color somehow suited him, and his piercing gray eyes sparkled. "It's good to see you."

Harrison's head bobbed slowly. "Yeah, you too. But it looks like you're busy." A quick glance at the bustling salon told Harrison that even a Tuesday afternoon saw a steady string of customers.

But Nolan shook his head. "Oh no, not at all. I'm almost done with this client. Give me about ten minutes. Angel, can you get Mr. Crawford something to drink?"

The front waiting area had comfortable chairs, so Harrison settled into one and pulled out his phone. Two games of solitaire later, he overheard Angel's voice at the front desk. "Would you like to schedule your next appointment with Nolan?"

The woman at the counter tucked her newly styled shoulder-length waves behind her ears and offered Angel her credit card. After she made her appointment for six weeks in the future, Harrison grinned. Nolan appeared to be every bit as in demand as he'd expected.

"Mr. Crawford?" Angel beckoned him with her hand, and he followed her to Nolan's chair. They passed other stylist chairs, filled with clients in various stages of hair styling, with more soft chatter coming from the manicure stations.

"Here he is." Nolan thanked Angel and then gave Harrison a quick once-over and adjusted the chair to his height. "I'm so glad you came," he said, and patted the chair. He reached into a drawer and pulled out a fresh cape, then set it on the counter. "How are you today?" he asked as Harrison sat down.

Something was off with the younger man. Nolan hadn't seemed this anxious when they'd met in his office, or even when they drove down the street where the accident had taken place. But here, in Nolan's salon, on his home turf—Nolan looked spooked. *Was he nervous?*

Coming here today had been a mistake. "I don't want to bother you. It's just—" Harrison pointed at his hair and shrugged. "I was on my way to see my barber and remembered your offer. But if you're busy, and it sounds like you are—"

"No." Nolan put his hands on Harrison's shoulders, and he froze at that touch. Their eyes met in the large mirror in front of Nolan's station. "I don't have any other clients right now. I took the afternoon off, and I'm done for the day.

Please, Mr. Crawford, I meant it." He swallowed. "I'd like to do your hair."

"Only if you're sure. And I told you to call me Harrison." Harrison's heart raced the entire time Nolan's hand rested on his shoulder. This was a mistake. The large mirror in front of him didn't help—the pink flush of Harrison's skin went from his cheeks to his chest, just at that simple touch. How was he going to manage an entire hair cut? But the die was cast. Nolan smiled again, and this time Harrison smiled back, and relaxed into the chair as best as he could. "You said you had some ideas for my hair. Do you think I need to get rid of this gray?"

Nolan reached for a comb and looked more intently at his hair. Then he gazed into the mirror at Harrison's reflection, and Nolan's fingers shifted the strands of hair this way and that, deep in thought. Finally— "Not a chance. You are not allowed to touch these silver tresses."

That flowery description made Harrison giggle. "It makes me look old, doesn't it?"

Nolan shook his head. "Not in the least. You look amazing." His fingers tugged lightly at the sides, checking for length. "Okay, let's get you shampooed and then we'll make some magic happen."

If Harrison had worried about embarrassing himself when Nolan touched his hair, he almost lost it at the shampoo station. Leaning back against the sink, all the tension he carried in his shoulders ebbed away with the warm water that rinsed his hair. So good. Then Nolan's fingers massaged his scalp and rubbed the soapy shampoo into his hair and—oh no. Harrison's cock decided this was a good time to make an appearance.

Thankfully, the voluminous salon cape wrapped around his body and hid his erection.

It was embarrassing, getting hard like a teenager, but when was the last time someone touched him with such care? Harrison couldn't remember. Eyes closed, he exhaled, all his breath released from his lungs, and he couldn't help the soft groan that escaped when Nolan's nails raked his scalp. It seemed to last forever, and yet it was over too soon. Harrison sat back up as Nolan towel-dried his hair. "Are you ready?" he asked.

Harrison's pants were uncomfortably tight. "Yes. Lead the way."

Back in Nolan's chair, the younger man studied Harrison's reflection in the mirror again, but now Harrison just watched Nolan's face, his hands. Those magic fingers ran through his hair again. "I want to take some off the sides, give you a low fade, but leave the top a little longer. You really do have great hair, all this body and wave. So many men would kill for hair like this." Nolan picked up his scissors and went to work. "What are your feelings on a three-day stubble look?" Nolan asked as he cut, an adorable look of concentration on his face.

Harrison snorted. "I don't know. When I grew up, they taught me that men shaved every day to look professional."

Nolan rolled his eyes, then turned the chair, and now Harrison faced away from the mirror. "Okay, I get that. But I think you could pull it off, some light whiskers down here. Done properly, that would look professional too."

"Won't it make me look old?"

The chair spun back until Harrison faced Nolan, the two of them staring at each other. "Why are you so worried about looking old?" Nolan asked.

"Because—" Was this the time or place to explain the beating he'd taken emotionally over the last few months? But this felt like a safe place. Harrison swallowed. "I feel old."

Bless him, Nolan just stared back with confusion written all over his handsome face. "But you're not old. What are you, forty-one? Forty-two?"

"Forty-six in August." Saying the words aloud made the gulf in their ages even more real.

Unperturbed, Nolan grinned. "That's not old. That's just getting started." The chair swung back around, hiding Nolan's face from Harrison again. "So, you're getting back into the dating scene. Have you met anyone you like?" he asked, scissors snipping around Harrison's ears.

Yes, I have, Harrison thought. "Not really. I've been busy with work, and I don't know how to get into those dating apps. My assistant is always threatening to set one up for me."

"Be careful with some of those dating sites. People aren't as honest as they should be."

"That's what I'm afraid of," Harrison admitted. "Back when I was younger, it was so much simpler. We just went out to a bar or a club, and if I saw someone I liked, I walked over to her—or him." Harrison paused. Had Nolan caught that hint? Why had he even brought it up? "If they were interested, you hung out. If they weren't, you found someone else."

Nolan's eyebrows raised when Harrison mentioned an interest in men. "So, if you don't like dating apps, it sounds like your plan is to stick to the tried-and-true methods. Does this mean we can expect to see you over Delirium one of these evenings?" Nolan pulled out a small razor and tidied up the back of Harrison's neck. "You should stop by, especially after I'm done with you. This style is going to look great."

"I'd be that old guy hanging out in the club." An image popped into Harrison's head, and he frowned.

"First off, you're not old. Stop saying that. Second, there's nothing wrong with someone being that old guy in the club. The olds need love too." Nolan chuckled, and Harrison's chair turned back and faced the front. "Third, a lot of people out there like older men, and not as a second choice or anything. Being with an older man can be hot, especially a gorgeous hunk like you."

Just then Nolan's cheeks reddened, and he dropped his eyes. *Does he feel it too?* He removed Harrison's cape and turned him to face the mirror. He brushed some hair off of Harrison's shoulders and grinned. "No fancy Italian suit today?"

Harrison laughed. "No, I took the day off to run some errands, and thought I'd stop by."

"I'm glad you did." Nolan took a deep breath. "Okay, we're done. Tell me what you think."

Nolan was right—leaving it longer on the top would leave more silver in, but the style was youthful enough that Harrison didn't appear older. He stared at his reflection, not recognizing the wide smile that broke across his face. "You were right." Their eyes met again. "You are amazing at this."

Nolan's bright smile was back as well. "You really like it?" he asked, his gray eyes shining.

"I do."

Nolan leaned against his counter, his posture relaxed again. "I enjoyed cutting your hair. Thanks for trusting me."

"No, thank you." Another one of those long looks passed between them. *Did we both feel this?* Had Harrison been out of the scene so long he didn't recognize this ache in his chest?

But it was time to go.

Nolan had worked Harrison into his schedule, and if he took the afternoon off, he probably had somewhere else he had to be. Finally, he stood up and Nolan walked him to the front counter. But when Harrison pulled out his wallet, Nolan waved it away. "This was on the house. It's a gift, a way of saying thanks for helping out my roomie."

Harrison objected immediately. "Please let me pay you for this."

"Nope." His lips curled and his chin tilted up.

Harrison had lost this fight. "Then at least let me leave you a tip."

Nolan pointed at the communal tip jar next to the register. "I don't need anything. Spending time with you made my day." Someone in the back of the salon called Nolan's name, and he turned his head toward it. "I better run. Thanks for coming in again, Harry, and let me know when I need to show up for the official deposition."

Harry. Harrison's face got hot, but he held it together. "Will do. Thanks again."

Nolan walked off. A low cough brought Harrison out of his trance. Angel had been standing next to them the whole time, wearing a soft grin on her face. "Do you want to schedule an appointment to come back?" she asked.

"Yes, I do. How about four weeks from today?" Harrison said absently. She handed him a small appointment card, and as he opened his wallet to slide it inside, he pulled out five twenty-dollar bills and dropped them in the tip jar.

Her jaw dropped.

They were precious, all of these kids. "Y'all have a great afternoon," Harrison told her, then left the salon and headed back to his house .

Chapter 7

On a good day, it took Nolan about twenty-five minutes to drive to his mother's place in northwest Houston. But because he left the salon late, he battled the start of rush hour traffic, and the trip was just under an hour. When he pulled up in front of her new house, Noah's Prius was already there, along with a few other cars that belonged to friends who worked in dog rescue with his mom.

Nolan corrected himself—he still called it his mom's new house, but it wasn't really new; she'd had it about seven years now. After high school, Noah and Nolan had moved away into an apartment together, so Dani Reynolds sold their childhood home and bought this place—a fixer-upper ranch-style house with a wraparound porch that stood on two acres of land, where she could keep more animals without getting into trouble with her neighbors.

Nolan opened the gate to her front yard and headed inside the house. Following the sound of voices, he found his mom and two of her dog rescue friends in the back of the house in the room she called her Puppy Palace, where she always brought her littlest arrivals. They all sat on the floor, talking and laughing. Dani's eyes brightened when she saw her son. "There you are, sweetie."

"Hey Mom," Nolan said and entered the room. "Sorry I'm late."

Dani stood and stepped outside of the large penned-in area and hugged him tight. "It's so good to see you, Nolan. Look what Ella and Roxanne brought me today. Aren't they adorable?" she asked and pointed at the pile of wriggling black and white puppies, each with a small colorful collar.

Nolan counted six. "They're cute." He knelt to pet them. "And they look healthy. How old are they?"

Ella looked up from her phone, her long blonde hair pulled back into a ponytail. "Almost four weeks." Ella and Roxanne were married and ran End of the Rainbow Rescue, the organization where Dani volunteered, and they'd all become close friends. "Your mom's going to foster them until they're ready to be adopted."

"That won't be long. Look at how cute they are. Where's their mom?" Nolan asked, turning his head. There wasn't an adult dog with the puppies, but these babies were too young to be on their own.

Roxanne laughed and ran a hand through her short black hair. "She's outside getting a break from these guys. They're weaned, but they still harass her. The poor old girl needs a break from them."

"She and I will have plenty of quiet time," Dani said, and sat back down in the large pen. A puppy immediately climbed into her lap. "Your brother's outside with Doctor Chance if you want to go say hello."

Nolan stopped by the kitchen and grabbed a soda before joining Noah and Chance out on the large back patio, where they played fetch with a border collie and Dani's old collie mix, Lucy. "Hey there." Nolan pulled up a patio chair to join them. The dogs paused their game long enough to greet him, then headed back out into the yard doing zoomies past the fence that led to the chicken coops, Dani's latest project. "I guess this is the mom?"

Noah nodded. "Yeah. Twenty bucks says Mom keeps her."

Nolan shook his head. "She's too spirited. Mom likes the lazy animals. That girl needs a family with some kids."

"Maybe. You missed all the fun, though. We got those puppies settled in. Chance here checked them out, and we helped deworm them." Noah wrinkled his nose. "That wasn't as awful as it sounds."

Chance, still wearing his blue veterinarian scrubs, laughed. "How are you doing, Nolan?" Chance Edwards was a veterinarian they'd met through the rescue organization. Ridiculously handsome with golden hair and a movie star smile, Chance had become a good friend to both the twins and their mother.

Noah interrupted before Nolan could answer. "How come you're late?"

Nolan shrugged. "Last minute client showed up for a cut and style." He should have stopped there, but as usual, his big mouth didn't shut up. "He's the guy helping Diego out, so I didn't want to say no, you know?"

"The lawyer? The one with the Mercedes?" Noah sat up and snorted. The penetrative glare he aimed in Nolan's direction bothered him, as if Noah read his mind. "Yeah, that's why you did it. Some sense of *obligation*."

"I don't know what you mean." Nolan ignored the way Noah emphasized that last word.

But Noah wouldn't leave it alone. "It's okay, brother. He was pretty cute if you're into older men."

Chance grinned, his head swinging back and forth like a tennis match. He was an only child and always enjoyed their petty quarrels. "Cute? Or handsome?" he asked and took a sip from his soda. His blue eyes twinkled with mirth. "I can get into a handsome older guy. But at a certain age, cute just gets annoying."

Nolan turned his body toward Chance and ignored Noah. "One might describe him as handsome, especially now that I've fixed up his hair. I did a great job." There it was again, that nervous babbling, so Nolan changed topics. "Did you guys know that Smokey and Bandit are named after movie characters?"

The answer was yes, Nolan judged from their loud cackles. "Oh Nolan, it's a good thing you're so pretty." Noah reached over and messed with his hair. "You can be so dumb sometimes. You didn't know that?"

"Ah," Chance shook his head. "In his defense, it's a pretty old movie, and Nolan's not interested in old things like that."

"I can think of one old thing he might be interested in," Noah said. He nudged Nolan's foot, so Nolan punched him in the arm. "Ow—fuck, that hurt. I'm telling Mom on you."

Later that evening, Nolan helped his brother take individual photographs of all the puppies so he could add them to the rescue organization's website. Nolan had to admit—Noah took brilliant pictures, showing each dog's personality, giving them their best shot at being adopted. After they finished that task, the brothers headed to the kitchen and washed their hands before dinner. "When are they up for adoption?" Noah asked their mother as he sat back down at the kitchen table with his laptop.

"They'll be ready to head out four weeks from today," Dani answered. A pan of spaghetti sauce simmered away on the stove, and Nolan pulled out plates and utensils as she stirred the sauce. "That reminds me, Nolan, how are your fellas doing? They'll be ready for adoption soon too, right?"

Nolan nodded. "They're great. But I think Diego's gotten attached to them."

"Aww." Dani's face dropped. She pouted her lip at Nolan and went back to drain the spaghetti. Giving up the dogs that stayed with them always hurt a little, but it was even harder when a special bond formed between the dogs and their foster parents. "How's the trial going? Has that awful woman dropped the lawsuit against Diego yet?" Diego's parents lived in Mexico, and he didn't see them often. Over the years, Dani had grown protective over their friend.

Nolan shook his head. "Not yet. She found herself a sleezy personal injury attorney who's got her thinking she'll make some good money out of this case."

"But Diego's got a lawyer of his own, right?" she asked and pulled a green salad out of the fridge.

"Yeah, and a good one." Nolan ignored the pointed look Noah shot in his direction, even as his face got hot. "He doesn't specialize in personal injury, but he's good at what he does." *Why did I say that?* "He's very reputable."

"Reputable," Noah murmured. But Dani caught the ugly glance between them, and they stopped.

After they plated their dinner and sat down at the table, the abuse continued. "Mom, Nolan didn't know *Smokey and the Bandit* was a movie," Noah said, and took a bite of his dinner.

Dani frowned. "Really, sweetie?"

Unbelievable. "When in my life would I have learned about this?" Nolan added some salad to his plate and sighed. "I don't recall being shown this when we were young."

Dani bit her lip. "You might have a point. It's my fault," she said to Noah, and they laughed. "What else is going on with you two?"

"I've finished the proposal for my dissertation." In addition to teaching world history to college freshmen, Noah was also working on his PhD. "And next week is spring break for the university, so I want to get started on it, but I've also got a lot of grading to do all week. The students had tests and I get to grade a couple hundred essays on the French Revolution."

"But that sounds like two things you love most—reading about boring history topics and being judgmental," Nolan said, and avoided the wadded-up napkin Noah tossed at him. Dani frowned like she did when they were little and fought with each other, but Nolan could tell she thought it was funny, too.

Noah just rolled his eyes. "At least I've got something I'm doing."

Ouch. Maybe it was time to tell them about the half-finished college application Nolan had been working on. On the other hand, maybe waiting was better. Why get his mother's hopes up again if he wasn't accepted?

Besides, Nolan grumbled as he took another bite of dinner—nothing he ever did seemed to compare with Noah's accomplishments. "Chance said that the rescue's got a fundraiser coming up."

Dani's eyes lit up. "Yes. We're teaming up with the Valley View Pride Center and a couple of other organizations for a big outdoor event at Buffalo Bayou Park next month. Noah, I volunteered your services to get some online promotions started." Then she turned and gave Nolan a sweet smile. "Nolan, I hoped you'd be able to help me that day with setting up."

He reached out and touched her arm. "Of course. I'd love to. Just let me know what day you need me."

And he meant it. But inside it simmered, that ugly notion that his talents weren't as important as Noah's, that what Nolan brought to the table would always be less impressive.

Dani seemed to know what Nolan was thinking and reached over to rub his arm. "Are you alright? Worried about the trial?"

"I'm fine," Nolan told her and smiled back. "Like I said, Diego's in the best hands." This time, when Noah raised his brow at Nolan, he met that steely gaze with one of his own.

No one was going to make him feel bad about Harrison.

Chapter 8

So many people at the law office had mentioned Harrison's haircut that by lunchtime, he felt self-conscious walking around. But every comment had been complimentary, and whenever he spotted his reflection in a mirror his chest tightened at the memory of Nolan's fingers in his hair, the tender way Nolan massaged his scalp, and the uncomfortable erection he'd endured on the walk back to Nolan's salon chair.

Spending time with Nolan was such a treat. The past year had been filled with his failing marriage, the divorce, and throwing himself into work. But these last few days, being around Nolan, reminded Harrison that maybe life wasn't over quite yet.

Maybe, in some ways, life had just begun.

Alicia knocked on Harrison's door and tore him out of those thoughts. "Just a reminder that you've got lunch with Judge Keller in an hour."

Harrison blinked. "Thanks, that slipped my mind."

Alicia glanced down at his desk. "And you neglected to jot it on your fancy calendar."

Harrison laughed at that gentle tease. "Thanks. Her office or mine?"

"Hers. One of her clerks called and asked me what deli sandwich you liked. I ordered you a turkey club with chips.

I figured it would be less messy than your usual Reuben, since you've got a meeting with the partners later this afternoon."

Always so thoughtful. "Sounds good. Thanks for looking out for me."

Alicia's warm smile lit her face. "Always, boss."

The Honorable Donna Keller's office was on the third floor of the county courthouse, three blocks from Harrison's office. He walked down the busy street to the courthouse, a lightness in his steps, and he even bypassed the elevator and jogged up the stairs to the third floor where the judge's chambers were located.

One of the clerks led him back to her chambers, where the dark leather chairs and dark wood desk were offset by touches of her native New Orleans, masks of purple, yellow, and green hanging from the walls. "Harrison. It's good to see you." Donna Keller stood just over five feet tall with short black hair and a bright smile but had a reputation for running a no-nonsense bankruptcy court. She rose from her desk to greet him, and glanced up at his hair, her lips curled in a smirk. But she didn't mention it. "How are you doing?"

Like most people, she'd worried about Harrison's emotional state since the divorce. Of course, everything had changed in the last week, and the end of his marriage was the last thing on his mind now. "I'm great." She shot him an incredulous look, and he belted out a genuine laugh. "Really."

"Well, we're gonna have to talk about that." Donna led him through a door to an adjoining conference room, where their lunch was spread out on a long mahogany conference table. "One of these days, I'm gonna wise up and go get a corporate job so I can get a big corner office like you." They sat and unwrapped their deli sandwiches. "Okay, 'fess up. What's with the haircut?" she asked, then took a bite.

"Why is everyone asking me about my hair?" There was more than a hint of frustration in Harrison's voice as he lifted his sandwich to his mouth.

Donna rolled her eyes. "Harrison Crawford, I've known you since law school and I don't think I've ever seen you do any more than run a comb through it. But this—" Donna pointed at him. "This looks nice. Add that to the fact that you're newly divorced and back on the market, which leads this jurist to deduce that you've met someone."

Oh. That wasn't what Harrison had expected, but in hindsight, it made sense. It wasn't just his haircut behind the grins and comments at his office.

They all assumed Harrison was seeing someone.

That Harrison was fucking someone.

"So, are you going to tell me her name?" Donna's question pulled Harrison out of his thoughts. "Or do I have to call Alicia and needle it out of her."

"I'm not seeing anyone. Honestly." Donna narrowed her eyes. "But—" Harrison paused and took a deep breath. "I did meet someone. It won't go anywhere, but just—" How to explain the way Nolan made him feel, how just spending time with him filled Harrison with joy—and other emotions. "It felt good to be flirted with again, you know? To feel wanted."

Donna touched his arm and gave him a gentle squeeze. "You're a handsome man, Harrison. It won't take long for you to find someone if you want to date again." She smiled wryly and reached for a potato chip. "Or have you already found that person? Do you want to tell me about it?"

Donna had always given him good advice and lent an ear (and a shoulder) when Harrison needed to vent about his marriage falling apart. They'd known each other for over twenty years, and he trusted her.

Still, nerves flooded through him as he spoke the words aloud. "His name is Nolan."

Her eyes widened slightly, and she picked up another potato chip, put it in her mouth, and chewed slowly. "Is he cute?"

Harrison exhaled, and all the tension slid off his shoulders. Of course, Donna understood. "He's so cute." Harrison broke out into a sappy grin. "I can't remember the last time I felt like this."

Her soft brown eyes met his. "Oh, you're smitten. That's adorable."

Harrison's face flushed with embarrassment. "I'm too old to be smitten. It's ridiculous."

"Nonsense. Does he feel the same?" Now that she knew, Donna was fully invested in his romantic situation.

Did he feel the same? His soft drink hovered in front of his lips for a long moment before the words spilled out . "I don't know. He's young. Way too young for me, and I genuinely think he was just being nice to me, you know? Flirting with the old guy, to make me feel good about myself." Harrison pointed at his head. "He gave me this haircut."

"It looks good. But why do you think he was just being nice to you? Like I said, you're not ugly, you know that."

Harrison slumped. "I'm too old for him. For God's sake, he's Troy's age."

Donna nodded sympathetically. "Okay, so that's a bit of an age gap. Let's start from the beginning." She pushed the remnants of her lunch away from her and rested her elbows on the conference table, her chin in her hands. "Tell me how you met. Spare no details."

Well then. Harrison explained how Nolan was involved in one of his cases, and how they'd spent some time together one afternoon while Harrison did some pre-trial investigating of the scene of the accident. "You should see these kids and their neighborhood. It's all so open now, walking around and holding hands. Being open about their sexuality."

"A lot has changed in the last twenty years. Did Jenny know about this?" Donna asked.

Harrison nodded. "She knew. I never acted on those feelings, never once in my life. But... she knew those feelings were there. That I'm bisexual." Harrison straightened in his chair as he spoke the word aloud. "I guess that's what they call it now."

Donna reached out and gave him a tight hug. "I'm glad you told me." She leaned back in her chair. "Are you going to be open about it at work and with your family?"

Her question was one that Harrison asked himself a dozen times since he met Nolan. "I don't know. I wasn't looking to date, honest I wasn't. That was the furthest thing from my mind after Jenny left. And if I hadn't met Nolan —" Would he be looking for love? Or still just moping around his big house by himself? "I don't know."

"I guess there's no real hurry, right? Why not test the waters with your Nolan, and see how it goes? After the trial, of course," Donna added.

Of course. But Harrison couldn't escape one notion that plagued his thoughts. "Tell me—am I crazy? Is this just some midlife crisis? I don't want to be that foolish man who goes out and buys a sports car and dates someone half his age to feel young again."

"I don't think this is crazy." Donna took another long sip from her soft drink, narrowing her eyes, deep in thought. "But you must ask yourself—is that all this is? An infatuation with youth? Grabbing the chance to be young again?"

That was the question. Harrison's shoulders shrugged. "I don't think so. I really like him, and not because he's in his twenties. He's funny and kind and makes me feel... interesting again. He thinks I'm cool. At least, that's how he makes me feel."

Donna's bright smile warmed him, but it was the affection in her eyes Harrison needed. She took his concerns seriously and understood what this revelation meant to him. "I don't see any harm in exploring these feelings, as long as they're mutual. No one would bat an eye if you dated a woman in her twenties. Hell, some of these old boys would be envious." She reached out and touched his hand. "It's good to see that smile of yours again. I've missed it."

Chapter 9

Very few things would have prompted Nolan to battle the traffic and drive downtown, but the certified letter he received in the mail the previous day had shook him to the core. Bold letterhead at the top of the thick paper announced it was from the law office of the attorney of the woman suing Diego, and the confusing legal verbiage sounded like she wanted to include Nolan in the lawsuit.

Diego and Nolan had both panicked, and Diego offered to call Harrison immediately and ask him. But Nolan wanted Harrison to see the letter in person and get it all straightened out, so he drove downtown as soon as work was done for the day.

Also—Nolan wanted to see Harrison again, even if it was just business. The look in Harrison's eyes when Nolan cut his hair, how Harrison watched his every move—the memory of it sent shivers down his back.

The same friendly receptionist as before greeted him. "How can I help you today?"

Nolan asked the receptionist if he could speak with Harrison Crawford.

Her brows furrowed. "Did you have an appointment, sir?"

Of course, Nolan's impulsivity had gotten the best of him again. He should have called first. Harrison had other important clients, or maybe he was in court today. *What was I thinking,* Nolan wondered, *walking in and demanding his attention?* "Um, no, I'm sorry. I don't, but—"

There he was. Harrison and another man walked together down a corridor toward the front lobby, their heads close in conversation. But as they got to the lobby, Harrison picked up his head and spotted Nolan. He straightened and said something to the other man, and then walked in his direction. "Hey. Is everything okay?"

Nolan held up an envelope. "I got this yesterday and wanted to show you."

Harrison thanked the receptionist and led Nolan back to his office. This time, instead of sitting in the comfortable conversation nook on the right side of the room, Harrison walked over to his large desk and sat down behind it. He pointed at one of the chairs in front of it and indicated where Nolan should sit. After Harrison slipped a pair of reading glasses on his eyes, he opened the envelope and pulled out the letter.

Sitting behind his desk, Harrison radiated professionalism, his demeanor businesslike. Nolan's hands curled in his lap. Was this the same kind, yet quirky man whose hair he had cut a few days before? "Am I in trouble?"

Harrison finished looking over the letter, concentration creasing his forehead as he read. Finally— "This is okay. They're asking for additional discovery from you. But we haven't had your formal deposition yet, so they can do it at the same time."

The knot in Nolan's stomach loosened, and he exhaled. "Are you sure? I showed it to my mom, and she said that she'd get me my own lawyer if I needed."

But Harrison shook his head. "I don't think that's necessary. This is an attempt to scare you, to get you to contact their office and meet with them alone, without benefit of counsel. They're hoping you'll say something different that they can use against Diego." He folded the letter and tucked it back into the envelope. "You were right to bring this to me. I'd like to make a copy for my records, but you should keep the original with the rest of your legal paperwork." He pressed on a button and asked his assistant to come into the room.

Nolan's head was still swimming. "So, I can just ignore it? Nothing bad will happen to me?"

"That would be my recommendation. There's nothing in here that compels you to contact them, and in my professional opinion, that would only hurt Diego's case."

"I'd never want to do that." Nolan relaxed back into his chair. This was the best news he'd heard all day.

The door opened and a young woman entered. "Alicia, will you please scan this letter? Then email me a copy and add it to Mr. Duarte's case file?"

"Absolutely, Mr. Crawford." Her curious eyes settled on Nolan for a moment before she turned and left the room.

But now Nolan felt foolish, rushing over and demanding Harrison's attention for something that hadn't been that important after all. "Okay, so I won't worry about this. Thank you for taking time from your day to help me." His eyes dropped to his hands, and a shy smile covered his face. "I'm a little embarrassed now, rushing down here and barging into your office."

But Harrison shook his head vehemently. "I'm glad you came. You didn't know what they were asking, and please know—I'm always open to talk to you anytime." Now it was his turn to reach for a business card off his desk. "I know Diego has my information, but this is for you." He scribbled something on the back and handed it to Nolan. "That's my cell phone, just in case the office is closed."

Nolan's fingers closed around the card, his heart pounding fast in his chest. "Thanks," he whispered, and tucked it into his pants pocket. "While I'm here, can I ask you about the real deposition? When is it? I just want to get it over with."

Harrison looked at his computer screen and clicked on the mouse a few times. "It's set for two weeks from today. But don't be nervous. You'll be great. And—I'll be right there next to you the whole time."

Harrison's eyes met Nolan's and held steady. "You do not know how good that makes me feel." They stared at each other for a long moment , but it wasn't uncomfortable.

A knock at the door interrupted them, and the same young woman walked in and handed Harrison the envelope. "Scanned and emailed. I'm heading out now, Mr. Crawford. Do you need anything else before I leave?"

"We're good. Have a good night." Her eyes lingered on Nolan again before she turned and left. "Was there anything else you wanted to ask about?" Harrison asked as he passed Nolan the envelope.

Nolan set it on the desk and shook his head. "I've taken up enough of your time." Just as he stood, a photograph behind Harrison's desk caught his eye. "Is that Troy?"

Harrison smiled and pointed at a framed picture of a young boy holding up a fish that he'd just caught. "Yeah, he's about ten there."

Next to it was a photo of Troy's high school graduation. A tall blonde woman stood next to Troy, with her arm wrapped around him. "Is that your—is that Troy's mother?"

Harrison nodded. "That's Jenny, my ex-wife."

The woman who let this man slip away. "How long have you been divorced?" Nolan asked and turned back toward Harrison.

"She left eight months ago. Officially divorced—" Harrison looked down at his calendar. "About a month now. But it was over a long time ago—years, and we both knew it."

All around the same time as Nolan's own break-up, and the accident that followed. "I guess we both had a shitty start to the new year," he said.

"I suppose you're right. But—I think things have been looking up lately, at least for me." Harrison laughed. "I can't tell you how many compliments I've had on my haircut. Probably more than in the whole ten years I've been here at this law firm. You did an excellent job."

Nolan's face heated at the compliment. Harrison had that effect on him. "I didn't do anything but show you what you look like. You're an incredibly handsome man." Now that his concerns about the letter were gone, Nolan relaxed in the other man's company. *Time to do some fishing.* "I'm sure whoever you're dating now tells you that all the time."

Harrison rubbed the back of his neck. "Oh, I'm not dating anyone."

Unbelievable. "Too soon?" There was no way someone hadn't snatched up this man as soon as he was available. Successful, powerful men like this never had to be alone unless they chose that.

"No, it's not that." Harrison glanced at the clock on his desk, then back up at Nolan with a curious gaze. "Seeing as it's now after five—" He opened a drawer in his desk and pulled out a bottle of liquor and two small glasses. "Would you like a drink?"

Holy shit. Nolan had seen people do this on television— take a bottle of expensive booze from their desk, and drink at work. It looked so fucking cool. "Yes please." Harrison poured two fingers of an amber liquid into each glass and offered one to him. Their fingers touched, and it set Nolan's skin on fire. "So, if it's not too soon to date, then why haven't you gone out with anyone?" he asked and tried to appear cool and composed.

"It's complicated." Harrison took a sip of his drink, then shook his head. "No, it's not complicated. I'm just scared."

Not the answer Nolan expected. "Of putting yourself back out there?"

"Of being honest with myself." Harrison took another sip, and then set his drink down. "May I ask you a personal question?"

Nolan nodded, surprised and curious. What had this man so deep in his thoughts? "Go for it."

Harrison tapped his fingers on his desk for a moment, fidgeted nervously. "How old were you when you came out? When you told people you were gay?"

There it was. Nolan leaned back in the chair and looked up, memories crashing through his thoughts. "It was a little easier for me at the time because I had my brother, Noah. He's queer too, and we both always knew about each other, you know? One day when we were thirteen or fourteen, he just asked me if I was ready to talk about it to our mom, and I said yes." Nolan lifted the glass and took another sip, then held it in his hands. "Mom seemed a little shocked that it was both of us—I tended to be the more flamboyant one, I guess. She'd pegged me as gay from childhood. The only thing that surprised her about my news was that I identify as bisexual. I like girls too. But Noah's strictly here for the D." Nolan tried to wheedle a smile out of Harrison with that last comment, but Harrison's impassive face was like a mask. "And that's my story."

"But your family was okay with it? And your dad? What did he say?" Harrison asked.

Nolan slumped a little in his seat, these feelings harder to explain. "Dad lives in Colorado. My folks split up when we were pretty young, and we don't see him often." Nolan didn't remember a lot of those days, back when they all lived together in Shreveport. After his folks split up, Dani moved her and the boys to Houston, where they grew up. "Since it was both me and my brother, the extended family seemed less inclined to think of it as 'going through a phase,' if that makes sense. And it wasn't like they could cut off the both of us. Most people seemed okay with it. Mom jumped on board and became a vocal ally. Dad—" Nolan shrugged. "He loves us, but he doesn't know us real well, so I'm not sure it changed our relationship one way or the other."

Harrison listened as Nolan spoke, his face still not betraying his thoughts. He'd be a great poker player. "I'm glad you and your brother had each other."

Nolan chuckled. "Me too. A lot of people, even a few teachers, thought that Noah was just pretending to be gay to make it easier for me. He's such a serious little grump. But no, the Reynolds boys were queer and ready to hit high school." It hadn't been easy, but they had friends and each other, and didn't have many of those horror stories that other queer people experienced. "And that's my story." But why had Harrison asked him that in the first place? Nolan pushed his luck and went out on a limb, hoping that Harrison would follow. "And you? What's your story, Harry?" Nolan asked and took another sip of the excellent scotch.

Harrison blinked and took a deep breath. His fingers touched and settled on his desk. "I'm attracted to women. But—I am also attracted to men and right now, there's this pull inside me to explore that." He exhaled after he spoke, as if the words had been a weight on him. "You're the second person I've ever shared that with, spoken those words aloud."

"I'm honored." It humbled Nolan that this man wanted to share that information with him, and he lifted his drink. "Welcome to the family."

Harrison did the same with his glass, a warm smile on his face. "You've helped me a lot in the last couple of weeks. Just talking with you and getting a glimpse of your life." Harrison shrugged. "I guess it showed me that a lot has changed in the last twenty years. Maybe I don't have to be so afraid of who I am."

This was a heady conversation that Nolan had not expected when he walked into Harrison's office that afternoon, but the more they talked, the more it felt as if they'd known each other for years. "And who are you?"

"I'm bisexual. At least, I think I am." Harrison ran his finger over the edge of the glass, and his face flushed. "I've never... been with a man, not like that."

"Never?" Harrison's admission was both surprising and sad. "Not even fooling around as a teenager?"

"Being gay wasn't part of my plan." Harrison looked around his office and waved his hand around. "I don't have any regrets about the choices I made back when I was your age. Jenny and I loved each other. At least we used to. But we grew apart."

Nolan took a quick sip of his drink. "That happens to a lot of couples, right? It doesn't always mean they divorce."

Harrison's brow furrowed. "No, it doesn't. And I would have stayed married if she hadn't left me."

Oh. Two thoughts hit Nolan at once—how much that admission surprised him, and how much that admission hurt him. "Were you happy with her?"

Harrison's eyes were dark and mournful. "I thought I was. I had what I'd always wanted—a big house, nice cars, a wife and kid. Money in the bank. That was supposed to be the magic ticket, right?" A bitter smile curled on his lips. It was the first time Nolan saw a cross look on his face.

He didn't like it. "Why did she leave?"

Harrison shrugged. "She wanted more than I could offer emotionally. Or she just grew bored with who I was."

"I can't believe that," Nolan said. How could anyone think this man was boring? "Did she know about you being bisexual?"

"She did. We never talked about it like adults, but she caught me looking at gay porn, or staring too long at an attractive man. But it was always something about me I tried to hide."

Nolan couldn't imagine hiding that part of him. His sexuality didn't define him, but it was an essential part of who he was. "I'm so sorry you had to live closeted like that."

That sadness in Harrison's eyes lifted. "Like I said, I don't regret my choices. Even though my marriage didn't last, I have a brilliant son. But now—" Harrison sat back in his chair and looked out the window at downtown Houston, and Nolan noticed that Harrison had taken his advice and had grown out some stubble on his face.

It looked great on him. "But now?"

"Maybe now I can see what I've been missing. Maybe it's not too late."

"Of course, it's not too late. You are not old." Nolan lifted his hand and began counting off on his fingers. "Harrison— you're handsome. You're successful, and incredibly intelligent. You're going to be beating them off with a stick, men and women." When Harrison stared at Nolan with this clueless, adorable look on his face, he wanted to lean over and kiss him, to show him how desirable he was—at least to Nolan. But this was Diego's lawyer, despite the incredibly personal conversation they just had. It had to stay professional... for now. "Just put yourself out there as soon as you're ready."

There was that sad smile again. "You make it sound so easy," he said, and finished his drink.

"It doesn't have to be hard." Nolan drank the rest of his scotch as well, the warm burn giving him courage. "I tell you what. Come out to Delirium with us this weekend. On Fridays they have theme nights, and I think this week is The Eighties."

Harrison laughed. "My kind of music?"

"I'm guessing you'll know a lot of the words." Nolan saw more of those walls breaking down around Harrison, and he liked the man behind them. Nolan liked him a lot. "At the very least, you'll know a couple of people there and won't feel like that creepy guy sitting alone at the bar. And if there's someone there that catches your eye—" It wouldn't take long for someone to swoop this man up, and if it couldn't be Nolan, then at least he could make sure that person wasn't someone shady.

"Friday night." Harrison arched a brow. "I admit, it sounds like fun. Are you sure I won't cramp your style? I don't want you to feel like you have to babysit me."

"Please." Nolan rolled his eyes to exaggerate his point. "Sitting next to a hottie like you will enhance my reputation. Also, I can tell people I did your hair. Free advertisement."

"Well, if you put it that way, I guess I have to go." Harrison looked down at his watch and whistled low. "I can't believe we've been talking so long."

Nolan glanced at his phone. Almost two hours had flown by. "Thanks for opening up with me."

"Thanks for listening. I had a lot to get off my chest," Harrison said.

An image of Harrison shirtless floated through his head, and Nolan bit his lip. "I'll see you Friday. Don't chicken out on me," he added, and stood to leave.

Harrison stood as well. "I'll be there, I promise."

Chapter 10

Yes, it was silly. Hitting the gym a few times before the weekend wouldn't make a drastic change to Harrison's physique or give him muscles overnight. But the previous evening, before he changed into his comfy sleeping t-shirt and shorts, he looked at himself in the bathroom mirror—a good, hard, objective appraisal. His broad chest and narrow waist hadn't changed much since his college days, but the definition in those muscles had worn away over the years. His chest hair started to turn gray a few years ago, just like the hair on his head, but it was still thick and soft. Harrison's fingers grazed across a nipple, and he inhaled sharply as it hardened, as sensitive as ever. A quick peek at his backside made him grin. That ass still looked good.

Overall, his first impression was 'Not bad for a forty-five-year-old dude.'

Second impression was 'Could be better.'

Beep beep.

Harrison's eyes blinked and adjusted to the dark as he tapped the alarm on his phone to shut off the incessant beeping. He let out a loud sigh. Was this *really* want he wanted to do each morning?

But an image of Nolan swam through his thoughts. *Yeah, okay, let's do this.* His legs swung over the side of the bed and he sat up, ready to hit the gym. As Harrison dressed in the work-out clothes he'd laid out the night before, a thought occurred to him—Troy might have left some weights in the garage. Hell, he could even turn one of the extra guest rooms into a private gym. But Harrison still paid for a family membership at a fancy gym that Jenny liked. Might as well try it out.

Dawn was still an hour away when he arrived. Harrison saw stars in the sky, but the fresh cool air invigorated him. The parking lot was a quarter full—another surprise. Inside the brightly lit gym, upbeat music blared from speakers in the ceiling, and after he fished an old membership card out of his wallet, a young woman at the front counter took it and examined it with a grin. "This is one of the old ones. Most people use the app on their phone to check in. Can I help you install that this morning?"

"Sure." Harrison handed her his cell phone and her fingers tapped away. She also gave him a smaller hang tag for his key chain, and after smartly observing that Harrison wasn't familiar with the gym, offered to walk him around and give him a quick tour. Initially, the plan was to hit the free weights and do some strength training with the barbells, but that part of the gym was more crowded than he expected, full of young people working on their muscles. Maybe not today. Instead, Harrison settled on the less-crowded weight machines.

His eyes darted around to see what other people were doing. Finally, he settled on a chest press machine and selected a lower weight to start with—no sense hurting himself by overdoing it on the first day. But it felt good, working those muscles that didn't see much action as he sat behind his desk at work. After the chest press, Harrison hit the lat pull-down bar, and then something for the biceps and triceps. The plan had been to focus on his arms, chest, and back, but the endorphins kicked in, and Harrison worked on his legs as well.

I'm going to feel this tomorrow. Maybe, but he stayed twenty minutes longer than he'd planned and enjoyed every minute.

The drive to work seemed less irritating. Breakfast was a banana and an apple instead of his usual cheese pastry, and he liked every song that played on the satellite radio and sang *Interstate Love Song* at the top of his lungs.

"Good morning." Alicia peered at Harrison with twinkling eyes when he energetically strode through the office. "Did you have a good night?" she asked and followed into his office.

"A quiet night, but a brilliant morning so far. What's on the agenda today?" he asked, setting his briefcase down on his desk. She handed him a thick file on an upcoming case and ran over the day's schedule. "Oh, he left it here."

"What?"

She held up Nolan's envelope. "Mr. Reynolds must have left it here. I'll have it mailed to him," she said, and added it to her clipboard.

"No. I mean—" Harrison almost blurted out that they'd be spending time together over the weekend. Instead, he held out his hand. "He'll be back in a few days. I'll give it to him then."

Alicia handed it to him with an interested expression, but she didn't press. "Interviews start at ten in the main conference room and last most of the day, with a break at one for lunch. They're ordering Chinese food, so I put you down for orange chicken and fried rice. Does that sound good?"

It did, but— "Would you change that to vegetables instead of rice?"

She nodded but arched a brow.

Harrison smirked. "My doctor, he wants me to make changes to my diet."

Alicia jotted it down. "Veggies, not rice. I'll let you know when they begin to gather."

After she left, Harrison settled at his desk, still holding Nolan's letter. *Nolan.*

His heart began to beat faster and those stupid butterflies fluttered in his stomach when he thought about Nolan, like some lovesick teenager. But just meeting Nolan and talking to him had changed so much about Harrison's life in just a few days. Harrison wanted to look better for him, to be better for him.

Harrison wanted him.

And Nolan wanted him, too, Harrison was sure it.

Not that anything could happen right now. Nolan was a part of a civil case that he oversaw, and ethically, it wouldn't be appropriate to pursue a relationship until the case was over.

But what if? What if something happened between them? Leaning back in his chair, Harrison smiled and fingered the envelope. Last night Nolan had been here, he'd sat in that chair right there and listened to him share his own personal story, then Harrison had opened up about his past.

At the very least, Nolan was fast becoming a good friend.

But Harrison wanted more.

"Mornin', Crawford." Ben Barton, one of the partners at his law firm, stood at the door and spoke in his usual slow drawl. The outward face of their law firm, Ben stood dressed head-to-toe in a western-style suit, complete with bolo tie and cowboy boots. But behind the handlebar mustache was one of the finest legal minds in the city. "We still on for ten?"

"Definitely. I hope we settle on someone today." Business boomed, and they needed another lawyer on their team to help relieve the ever-growing caseload.

Harrison selfishly had another reason for wanting to find someone soon. While he'd spent the last several months working late to avoid his emotional problems, something told him he might want his nights and weekend free from now on. "Main conference room?" he asked.

"Yep. I hope we find someone we like soon. It's just getting busier by the week." Ben turned to leave, then double backed around, his brow furrowed. "Everything been going okay with you?"

"Yeah," Harrison answered, surprised. He opened his mouth to ask why Ben was concerned, but then—oh, yes. The divorce and his recently depressed outlook. Had it just been a few days before that everything seemed bleak and gray, a long stretch of empty life ahead of him? Now all Harrison could imagine was a bright future, with potential for fun and laughter and spending time this weekend with a sexy young man who thought he was handsome. "I'm doing great, but thanks for asking," Harrison added with a genuine smile.

Ben's brushy eyebrow quirked, but his answering grin spoke volumes. "Good to hear, pal. We'll talk more later."

Chapter 11

"Can you believe it?" Diego tore apart his room, looking for his lucky hat. "We've been trying to get into Brewster's regular roster for months now and then all of a sudden—boom! I still can't believe our luck."

Sitting on the floor of his room, Nolan held Smokey and watched Diego packing extra clothes into his backpack. "Brewster's is a big deal, and on a Friday night? It'll be packed. But they're just lucky you guys weren't already booked somewhere else tonight and could step in when their other band bailed on them." The last-minute call for Steel Horse to fill in tonight had Diego more energized than Nolan had seen in months. "I hate to miss it."

"Me too." Diego paused long enough to frown at him. "You're sure you can't come? It would be amazing to get some video clips and pictures of us performing."

"You know that on any other night, I'd be there in a heartbeat. But—" Nolan bit his lip and bounced his knee up and down, which irritated the puppy, who jumped off his lap in a huff. "I kinda... told someone I'd be at Delirium tonight, and I don't want to flake out on them if they go."

Diego's dark eyes widened. "You met a guy?"

Nolan licked his lips. "Maybe. He's more like a friend—with possibilities."

"Please say it's not Jake." Diego sat down, his shoulders slumping. "I don't think I could handle another round of the Nolan and Jake Show."

"Oh, fuck no, it's not Jake." From the day Nolan met Harrison, Jake hadn't entered his mind unless someone else brought him up first. "Hope you guys break a leg, or whatever it is I'm supposed to say."

Nolan got up and headed into his bedroom to get ready. After a quick shower, he ran through the contents of his closet. The more he thought about it, the better it was that Diego wasn't going to Delirium tonight. He'd want them both to dress up in garish neon shirts and look like they'd come straight from some Eighties pop group, or like Boy George or something. On any other night, that would have been fun, and something Nolan might enjoy, but he hadn't figured out a way to tell Diego that he didn't want to look silly tonight.

Luckily, Diego left the apartment early to head to his gig, so Nolan had plenty of time by himself to make sure he looked good.

Just in case.

Nolan's mother had bought him a new shirt for Christmas, a light silky fabric in rich dark purple with short sleeves, and he hadn't worn it yet. A little tight in the chest, but that just meant that he needed to leave the top three buttons undone, right? Paired with some tight dark jeans and his favorite Sperrys, he looked pretty damn cute, if he said so himself.

A dab of styling paste rubbed into his hair for the perfect 'just rolled out of bed' look, and some smudgy kohl eyeliner to make his gray eyes pop, and Nolan was ready to go.

Even though Nolan arrived at the club earlier than usual, the parking lot was already half-full—always the sign of a good night. After a quick circuit around the club—the front bar, the back bar, the small patio, and the dance floor—to see who was there and who was working, Nolan found an empty stool at the back bar and started chatting with Grant, one of the bartenders. They were gossiping about one of the new barbacks when someone tapped on Nolan's shoulder.

"Hello, little brother." It was Noah. Great.

"Hey, you." Nolan reached out and hugged him, ducking out of Noah's reach when he lifted his hand to mess with his hair. Any other night, Nolan would love to see his brother at the club. Noah wasn't a regular here. He didn't go to clubs and out dancing with them all that often, but they always had a good time when they got together in this sort of setting. But tonight, the last thing Nolan wanted was for Noah to see him with Harrison and tease him about his silly crush on Diego's lawyer. "Surprised to see you here."

"Chance mentioned it. He should be here too, later. Oh, this is Martin." Noah introduced him to the man standing next to him. Martin looked to be Noah's type—dark, burly, and not very smart, which Nolan always thought was strange for a bookworm like Noah. They all chatted a few more minutes before the two of them ordered drinks and took off for the back patio area, and Nolan did another circuit around the club.

He's not coming. He had all but given up hope when—finally—Harrison walked into the club, and from the way heads turned as he strode inside, Nolan wasn't the only one who noticed him. Harrison had this presence about him that made people stop and look, and tonight he looked amazing. He wore a crisp, white, long-sleeve shirt rolled up to the elbows and dark khakis, and as he strolled, he took in the entire scene like an explorer documenting a strange new land. Harrison didn't see Nolan at first, but his eyes scanned the club, looking over the dance floor and bar until he found Nolan—and he smiled.

Nolan's heart raced—and his cock twitched—at that smile. It was electric. They walked toward each other, and Nolan greeted him with a friendly hug. "You made it."

"Yeah." For a moment, something clouded those chiseled features—not fear, but a hint of apprehension, as Harrison glanced up at the men in thongs gyrating on the raised platforms that surrounded the dance floor. "This is incredible." Then those bright blue eyes turned toward Nolan with a focused intensity that shook his insides. "You look great."

"This old thing?" Nolan playfully tugged on the collar of his shirt, but inside, he jumped up and down. *Harrison was here for him.* "Do you want something to drink?"

Harrison nodded. "Lead the way." They headed toward the back bar, where it was cooler and quieter. Heads turned as they walked, and it wasn't just because Nolan looked good tonight. The hot new guy was on his arm, and while the initial plan had been to introduce Harrison to new people and let him scope out the gay club scene, Nolan's personal plans had changed.

He would keep this man next to him as long as he could.

After they grabbed a couple of drinks from the bar, they found an empty table in the back to sit and talk. "So, what are your first thoughts? Everything you thought it would be?" What did all this look like through Harrison's beautiful eyes?

Harrison's face held this childlike expression of wonder. "It's loud out there, and more crowded than I thought it would be."

"Wait until we dance later." Nolan couldn't wait to get him out there and watch him move, but this was a lot to take in. *Baby steps.* "When was the last time you were in a place like this?"

Harrison shrugged. "A gay club or just out dancing in general?"

"Either. Both," Nolan answered with a smirk.

Harrison's eyes narrowed, deep in thought. "I went to a couple gay clubs in college, but that was mostly just with friends, and we were fucking around, you know? Just wanted to see what they were like. I would never have talked to anyone there or tried to meet someone. Hm, last time I was out dancing, that was about ten, twelve years ago? Maybe a little longer. By that time, I was married and had a kid, so it wasn't like we would go dancing too often. An occasional night out with other couples. Most social events were work-related, or things with my ex-wife's charitable organizations."

Nolan didn't like when Harrison talked about his ex-wife. It reminded him that Harrison had an entire life before they met. That made him feel petty. "Do you miss that?" he asked, sipping on his drink.

"Going out with my ex-wife?" Harrison asked.

Nolan nodded.

"Nope. Not even a little. It was fake, inauthentic. Looking back, I see how we were just pretending to be a happy family." Harrison's eyes wandered all around, watching men walking by holding hands, kissing each other. "I miss that." He pointed at a couple at the bar, clearly in love (if not lust) with each other, their faces close as they spoke. "That feeling you get when someone cares about you, and you just want to spend every minute of the day with them."

This felt like one of those moments in a romantic movie where the two main characters lean in and kiss, magical and cinematic. Nolan opened his mouth, not sure what he was going to say, but he wanted to tell Harrison that he could have anyone here in this bar, Nolan included, because Harrison was smart and sexy and confident and looked delicious in that white shirt with the rolled-up sleeves.

Nolan wanted to say that—but right then, at that moment, Noah showed up. "Hey, little brother." Fucking hell. He and Martin sat down next to them as Noah gave Harrison a quick once-over.

"Hey Noah." Nolan turned to Harrison. "You remember my twin brother, Noah?"

"Wait—" Martin glanced between them. "You're twins."

Jesus, Noah's taste in men never changed. "Yeah," Nolan said, his voice dripping with sarcasm. "Identical even."

Noah shot him a dark look. "Introduce me to your friend, little brother."

"Enough with the little brother, okay?" Nolan snapped at him. "This is Harrison Crawford, a friend of mine. You met him last week. Harrison, this is Noah, my brother, and his friend Martin."

Noah's eyes widened. "Diego's lawyer?" he asked.

"Yes sir." Harrison held out his hand. "Pleased to see you again."

Noah shook it and nodded. "I saw you the other day when I dropped Nolan off in the parking lot here."

"That's right." Harrison turned toward Nolan, his smile soft and sweet, before he finished answering Noah. "Your brother here's been helping me set things straight for Diego, getting his case organized. He's a good guy."

"Nolan's the best," Noah said. Nolan caught a hint of 'protective brother' in his words, and while he appreciated Noah looking out for him, tonight was not the night. "I don't think I've ever seen you here before."

"My first time here." Harrison's hand rested on his thigh, and while he spoke, his pinky finger slid over and pressed against Nolan's leg. "But not my last."

Oh shit, Nolan thought. The smallest touch, but so fucking possessive, and Nolan's heart pounded like a drum in his chest.

Just then, their friend Chance walked over, decked out like the teenager from *Back to the Future*, complete with puffy orange vest. "Heya." He frowned. "What, no one else dressed up?"

Noah cackled, and Nolan introduced Chance to Harrison. After a few moments, Noah, Martin, and Chance headed off to walk around.

Finally. Once they left, Nolan exhaled and hung his head back.

Harrison got up to get them each another drink. "So, what's the deal with you two?" he asked and handed Nolan a Cosmopolitan.

Nolan shrugged. Did he want to get into that strange family dynamic tonight? "You got any brothers or sisters?"

"A sister, but she's eight years older than me." Harrison caught Nolan's eye and frowned. "Not the same. You don't have to talk about it if it—"

"No, it's cool," Nolan said quickly. "It's not a problem. We just have normal brother problems, and normal twin problems, and probably normal gay guy problems, but just all rolled up together. I love him, and he's my best friend. But he's better at everything that matters."

"Not everything." Harrison nudged him with his shoulder.

Nolan snorted. "Feels that way sometimes."

Harrison hadn't moved away. Their arms pressed against each other, and Nolan's skin heated where they touched. Then Harrison stood, holding his hand out to Nolan. "C'mon. Show me around this place."

Nolan took the hand and let Harrison pull him up. "Sure thing." The crowd pressed against them, but Harrison kept Nolan close to him, holding his shoulder as they walked around the club, and Nolan pointed out people he knew.

"Noooolan." An elaborately painted drag queen strolled toward them, kissed Nolan's cheek, and stood back, as if examining him from head to toe. Delilah L'Amour stood six-foot-five in heels with hair teased to the ceiling. "You look scrumptious, darling. And who is this morsel?" she asked, and practically licked her lips as she explored Harrison's body with her eyes. She held out her hand for him to kiss. "Enchanté."

Harrison grinned and kissed her hand. "Ma'am."

"Oh, a gentleman." Delilah moved closer to him. "How refreshing in this den of sin to meet someone with manners."

Nolan slung a protective arm around Harrison's shoulder. "Back off, Delilah," he said playfully. "This gentleman is busy right now."

She pouted with great exaggeration. "Finders keepers? That's not fun. Well then, you'd better not misplace Harrison here, or someone else might make off with him."

"I doubt that," Harrison said, and his arm wrapped around Nolan. "But it was nice to meet you, ma'am."

Her face lit up. "Likewise," she said with a wink, and headed off to another table.

"Oh shit." Nolan laughed and ducked his head. "Did she just low-key threaten to kidnap you?"

"Sounded like it, and I think she could manage it with one arm tied behind her back, so you better keep an eye on me." Harrison finished his drink and set it on the bar. "Want to dance?" he asked.

"Hell yeah." Nolan finished his drink in one long swallow, grimaced at that powerful hit of alcohol, and they headed into the blaring loud main room.

The promised Eighties music turned out to be dance club remixes of eighties songs, each one blended into the next. Most of the songs Nolan recognized because his mom played them in her car when they were kids, or from the salon when they played older music.

The dance tempo stayed fast, and most people sang along to the music. Nolan caught Harrison singing along to a song, and moved closer to him, talking right into his ear. "Who's this?"

"Depeche Mode." Harrison swung his hips as he moved close to Nolan. "I saw them in concert in '93."

"I was born in '94," Nolan said, and bumped their hips together.

"Infant." Harrison rolled his eyes, but he laughed and pulled Nolan a little tighter against him. Nolan's hands reached for Harrison's hips, and they swayed together, finding a rhythm that suited them both. Harrison was a fantastic dancer, and even though Nolan still didn't know Harrison well, it looked like he was having a great time.

They danced and danced, and Nolan lost track of time, but just as he wiped a bead of sweat off his face, he saw Noah on the side of the dance floor. He beckoned Nolan toward him. "We're heading out, gonna try to catch Diego's second set. You two want to join us?" he asked.

It was tempting. Steel Horse always put on a good show. But Nolan had invited Harrison here tonight and didn't think bar hopping was a good first excursion out into the night life.

Also, Nolan didn't want to share Harrison with them, not just yet. "I think we're good here, thanks." Nolan looked over at Harrison. "Unless you want to go."

He shook his head. "Whatever you want."

Noah, Martin, Chance, and another friend they found waved and headed for the front door.

They danced to a few more songs, but after a while Harrison nodded his head away from the dance floor, and Nolan followed, his hand on Harrison's arm. They found a quieter spot in the back, but even here, the crowds had turned out tonight and there wasn't much room for privacy. "Want to get another drink?" Nolan asked.

Harrison shook his head and looked down at his watch. "I'm good."

Nolan's heart sank. "Do you need to go?"

Harrison nodded. "Pretty soon. I had a long day." But he'd had a good time, of that Nolan was certain, and that was what mattered.

This was Harrison's first outing in a queer setting in years, so Nolan counted it as a success. "I'll walk you to your car."

Harrison grinned. "You don't have to. Stay and have fun with your friends or go see Diego."

"I might go." Checking his pockets, Nolan felt for his keys and wallet, then reached for Harrison's hand and took it in his own. Crowds thronged around them, but all Nolan saw was Harrison's wide eyes staring at their locked hands. "But let's get you to your car first. I have to make sure Delilah doesn't make off with you."

Chapter 12

Even though they'd left the noise and bright lights of the night club behind as they walked toward the parking lot, the thumping bass still pounded in Harrison's ear.

Or maybe that was the sound of his heart beating in his chest.

The cool air felt fresh and invigorating after all that dancing, and Harrison couldn't remember the last time he felt this energized. The music, the people, the entire atmosphere screamed of youth and sex and passion. A pack of brightly dressed kids passed them on their way inside the club; their night of music and dancing just getting started. Yet here he was, ready to head home at midnight like Cinderella, trying to keep the carriage from turning into a pumpkin.

But Harrison had been at the gym early that morning and put in a full day of work—and it had been a long time since he was out late like this. His only regret was disappointing Nolan. "You don't have to walk me all the way out there." But Nolan's hand remained firmly tucked in Harrison's as they made their way through the jam-packed parking lot.

"I want to." After a few more steps, Nolan asked, "Tell me honestly—did you have a good time?"

As they reached Harrison's car, he turned and leaned against the passenger side and laughed. "God, yes. I can't believe you all do this every weekend. Even when I was your age, I think I had settled down like an old man."

Nolan shrugged, and that effervescent smile dimmed. "That's because you were a proper grown-up by my age. Noah calls all of this—" He spread his arms wide. "—my perpetual adolescence."

That family dynamic intrigued Harrison, but right now, more than anything, he wanted to see Nolan smile again. "Now you tell me, honestly. Are you happy right now?"

There it was. The corners of his generous mouth curled up. "Mostly. Right now, yeah."

"Then you shouldn't worry about what Noah or anyone else says." Voices came from the right, another couple leaning against their car, talking and kissing. But soon their make-out session got hot and heavy, and one man knelt in front of the other. "Um, do you want to talk for a little bit inside my car?"

Nolan glanced to the right and spotted them, too. "Yeah. But I thought you had to go."

"In a few minutes." Harrison's hand shook a little as he opened the passenger door for Nolan, and he slid inside. Heart thumping in his chest, Harrison walked over to his door and joined him inside the car. They sat a moment in darkness, but the lights from the parking lot illuminated Nolan's face. His chest rose and fell, still breathing heavy from the dancing and walking, and wispy chest hair peeked out the top of his unbuttoned shirt. He looked as unsettled as Harrison felt, and somehow that made him feel better. "Thanks again for inviting me out tonight and showing me around your hangout. I had a great time."

Nolan leaned back into the seat and turned his head toward Harrison. "Thanks for coming. Um—it meant a lot to me that you trusted me with this. Your first visit out to one of these places. I'll, um, let you know next time they do something special here."

Nolan's unexpected shyness brought out this protective feeling inside Harrison that had nothing to do with their age gap. "I think you're pretty special."

Nolan's eyes grew wide and shone in the dark.

Harrison wasn't sure who made the first move. He reached for Nolan's hand, and Nolan moved closer to him.

And then they kissed.

Soft kisses at first, just the lightest brush of lips against each other. Harrison hesitated, a hundred thoughts running through his head—*This is too fast. We need to slow down. Is this really happening to me?*

Then Nolan's fingers lifted his chin, and he kissed Harrison again, deeper, and all Harrison could think about was him.

Nolan's long arms wound around him, and Harrison pulled him closer, and somehow Nolan ended up on Harrison's lap, straddling him. One kiss turned into two, then another and another, each one hungrier than the one before. Harrison reached down and pushed his seat back as far as he could, so that the steering wheel didn't dig into Nolan's back, and his hands settled on Nolan's hips, holding him close. Harrison's erection pressed against Nolan's ass, and he ground down into it as his mouth found Harrison's neck.

Fuck, this was bliss. Harrison's hands cupped Nolan's ass and squeezed, delighted at the groan it elicited from him. Nolan's hard cock pressed against Harrison's stomach, and he wanted to touch it, to taste it, to make Nolan feel as good as he felt right now. Harrison's hand slid between their bodies, and he pressed his fingers against Nolan's denim-covered erection.

Nolan trembled with a low moan—and then stopped. "Wait."

Wait? Harrison froze, his hands immediately at his sides. *Had he done something wrong?* "I'm sorry," he murmured, and pushed Nolan back, embarrassed at whatever he had done. "I didn't—"

"No, no." Nolan cupped Harrison's face with his hands, and lifted it up to his, and kissed Harrison again, tender. "Not like this, not tonight. Your first make-out experience with a guy will not be in a car in the parking lot of some gay club." Nolan's long fingers ran through Harrison's hair, the lightest scratches on his scalp. "After tonight, if you still want me, if you still want to do this with me, we're gonna do it right. Proper."

Harrison's heart started to beat again. *We're gonna do it right.* "Of course I'll still want you, Nolan. You're the most beautiful man I've ever known."

Nolan's eyes sparkled in the dark, and they kissed one more time before Nolan slid off and shifted back over to his side of the car. "For the record, that was incredible, and you're a great kisser." He palmed at his hard cock, shifting it in his pants with a distressed groan. "Are you okay?"

"Raging boner aside? Yeah, I'm great." Harrison's balls ached, painfully full, but he reached out for Nolan's hand. "I won't tell you the last time I had a first kiss with someone."

"I probably don't want to know." Nolan leaned back against the seat, a satisfied look on his well-kissed face. "You're a great guy, Harry."

"You're incredible." They sat in the dark, holding hands. Harrison couldn't recall the last time he'd been so out of his element, and yet so happy. What did someone say at a moment like this? It had been twenty-five years ago when he'd courted someone. Did Nolan need anything from him? Did he expect something? Maybe he'd just done a good deed tonight, getting Harrison's feet wet, so to speak, and back into the dating scene. But Harrison hoped it was more. "Be careful heading home," he said.

"You too." Nolan leaned over for one more sweet kiss and then opened the passenger side door. Light flooded into the car, and Harrison blinked—and Nolan was gone. He walked toward his own car and for a moment, Harrison considered following him to see if he went home or out with his friends.

But Harrison needed to get home, and how Nolan spent the rest of his night wasn't his concern. At least not yet. One day, maybe, if the gods were kind to old men starting over.

Pulling out of the parking lot, Harrison headed left and went home.

Chapter 13

Lesson one about dating an older man—or at least Nolan's older man. Harrison wasn't big on texting.

The morning after they made out in his car, Nolan sent him a quick '*Good morning, handsome*' text after he woke up.

Three minutes later, his phone rang. "Hello there."

"Hi, hon. Are you busy?" Talking on the phone wasn't something Nolan particularly enjoyed. His mom was the only person he ever really called. But he could get used to listening to Harrison's low, growly voice.

"Not yet." Nolan stretched. He was still in bed since he didn't have to go into the salon until ten. "I'm getting ready to jump in the shower."

Harrison made a soft noise. "That's... that's quite the image, isn't it?"

Nolan grinned and rolled over onto his stomach, like a lovesick teenager, and hugged his pillow. The sheets tangled up against his legs. "I guess. Do you have a busy day planned?"

"Yeah, just puttering around the house. The garage is a mess, and I've been putting off cleaning it out. If there's any time left, I want to clean up the yard and get the pool ready for the summer. Somewhere in there, I oughta catch up on some work for later this week. I've gotta be in court at least three days this upcoming week. Um, that reminds me—" Harrison paused for a beat. "We've got depositions for Diego's case week after next, if I'm remembering right. Does that still work for you?"

Nolan closed his eyes, his stomach twisted up in a knot. Sometimes he forgot how he and Harrison met—the fucking lawsuit. "Just let me know when I need to be there. But do you think—" Nolan sat up and threw his legs off the side of his bed. "Do you think we can go over some of my testimony again? There's nothing improper about that, is there?" Nolan tried to sound as innocent as possible. On the other end of the phone, Harrison sighed. "I mean, I don't want to do anything wrong. We can wait—"

"No." Harrison interrupted him. "No, it's okay. Let's go have some dinner together tonight. Does that sound okay? We can talk about the case if you want."

"And if I want to talk about you?" Nolan wanted to hear that playful growl again.

Harrison chuckled. Close enough. "We can do that too. What time should I pick you up?"

His new sweetie was picking him up for a dinner date. Keeping the giddiness out of his voice, Nolan answered. "I'll be ready at seven."

"I'll see you then."

Saturdays were never slow at the salon, but this one flew by, Nolan's mood higher than the clouds in the sky. Once he made it back to the house, he stood in front of his clearly inadequate closet, filled with dozens of colorful shirts, all suitable for a Pride parade.

But maybe not a fancy steakhouse with his distinguished dinner companion. "What do you think, guys? Do I have time to go shopping?"

Smokey and Bandit ignored Nolan's predicament, so it was up to him to solve this problem. Harrison had already seen his one nice dress shirt when Nolan first visited his law office. Would the man care if he showed up in the same shirt? Probably not, but Nolan wasn't sure where they were going, and looking good was important tonight. Luckily, Nolan found something suitable in Diego's closet—a super soft crewneck sweater in deep maroon.

Diego wasn't around to ask, but he'd be okay with Nolan borrowing it—he was pretty sure.

One last glance at himself in the mirror as he checked his hair quelled his nerves. Presentable, yes. Nolan had pulled it off—first date casual chic.

His phone vibrated, and his nerves shot through the roof again. But it was just Noah.

Noah: *We're gonna go see that dinosaur movie tonight. Want to come?*
Nolan: *Got plans. I'll talk to you tomorrow.*
Noah: *What plans?*

As if Nolan would tell him.

He tucked his phone into his pocket and ignored Noah's last question. His brother would find out eventually, so why not just make it later? The last thing Nolan wanted right now was to hear Noah tell him what he was doing wrong, how he was fucking up his life, how inadvisable this crush was, with potential legal, moral, and personal repercussions.

Nothing Nolan hadn't thought about on his own.

Knock knock.

The sound shook Nolan out of his thoughts, and he glanced at his phone. Seven o'clock, right on time.

Opening the door to a gentleman caller sounded so old-fashioned, but that's how it felt when Nolan saw Harrison standing there in a dark blue shirt and chinos. "Hello, handsome." Nolan opened the door wide for him to step through.

"Hello." Harrison leaned in and pecked his cheek, then walked inside. His first glance was toward the dining room puppy area. "How are the boys doing?" he asked and stepped toward them.

"Growing like weeds." Nolan followed him and watched as Harrison knelt and pet their heads. "They're already getting some interest on the foster organization's website. It won't take long for them to get adopted."

"I hope they find great homes." Harrison stood and turned back to Nolan, his eyes darting all over his body. "You look great, by the way."

Nolan's shoulders shrugged as casually as he could manage. "Yeah, it's okay. I understand if you only want me for my dogs."

"Not just your dogs." Harrison grinned and stepped close enough that Nolan caught a whiff of his cologne. "Did you decide where you wanted to eat?"

Nolan grabbed his house keys and opened the door. "I had a couple of ideas. Do you like sushi?" Harrison made a face, and Nolan laughed as they headed to his Mercedes. "Okay, no sushi."

Harrison got to the passenger side before Nolan and opened the car door for him again, and Nolan's heart thumped faster. "No, let's go if that's what you want. I'm sure there's something I'll like." Harrison slid into his seat and turned on the car. "My assistant is always raving about this Japanese restaurant uptown, if you want to try it."

"Sounds great." Harrison pulled the car onto the street and soon they were on the highway heading north.

The first time Nolan was in Harrison's car, it was afternoon and they just drove the short distance between Delirium and his apartment, and Nolan spent most of the time talking about the accident. But tonight, as he leaned back in the plush leather seat, they cruised at seventy miles per hour down the interstate. Sirius XM's 90s on 9 satellite radio station played low in the background. *This is how rich people live*, Nolan thought. "Did I mention what a splendid car this is?"

Harrison grinned. "It's okay. I was thinking about getting something new."

"Is there something wrong with this one?" Nolan asked, his fingers sliding across the large touchscreen panel.

Harrison waved a hand. "I figured, if I'm having a mid-life crisis, isn't that what people do? Date someone younger and get an expensive sports car?"

"Is that what this is? You're going through something?" Nolan looked out the window and laughed, not sure Harrison was kidding. "Should I be flattered?"

"Oh absolutely," Harrison said, and reached for Nolan's hand. "Someone I trust implicitly told me I could date anyone I wanted. And I want you."

The darkness of the car kept Harrison from seeing him blush, but Nolan felt himself go bright pink. "Well, that's good."

It turned out that Harrison's assistant had excellent taste in Japanese restaurants. Nolan ordered an ahi tuna tower and a sushi roll made with snow king crab that was excellent, each mouthful more delicious than the last. Harrison ordered sea bass, and they split a bottle of plum wine and talked about their days like they'd known each other for years.

After dinner, they walked along the pedestrian trails at Buffalo Bayou Park, close to Nolan's place. "They always have a big celebration here during Pride month."

"Another first for me." Harrison nudged him with his shoulder. "I look forward to seeing it with you."

Two months in the future, and Harrison was making plans to be together. "It's a date," Nolan answered. His fingers tugged at Harrison's belt loop. "Want to head back to my place for a bit?" Nolan winced at the nervous twinge in his voice.

Harrison didn't seem to notice. He stepped closer to Nolan and touched his shoulder. "I'd like to," he said, his voice low and hoarse.

They made it back to Harrison's car and drove in silence to Nolan's apartment complex, then sat in the dark parking lot for a moment, neither one moving. Diego's car wasn't there. Good. "You okay?" Nolan asked when Harrison didn't open his car door.

"Yeah. Just a little nervous."

Nolan reached out his hand, and Harrison pulled it to his lips and kissed it. "Don't be. Nothing has to happen. Nothing will happen that you don't want."

"Maybe that's the problem." Harrison tilted his head, his eyes dark and needy. "I want it all."

"Greedy." Nolan leaned over and kissed him, then slid back and opened his door.

Harrison followed him into the apartment and looked around. "No roommate?"

"Working, I think. Saturday nights can get busy at the tattoo parlor." Nolan set his keys down and glanced over at the puppies, wriggling wildly when they spotted the men approaching. "Want to help me walk them before we…"

"Oh yeah." Harrison helped harness them, and they took the dogs out to the grassy lawn area behind their apartment and watched as they waddled around, sniffed around the grass and took care of business. Harrison sat down on a bench and played with Bandit, who rolled over and exposed his belly for rubs. Standing behind Harrison, Nolan put his arms around him and kissed the side of his head. Harrison's hands settled over his. But how could something so comfortable and warm make Nolan's heart race?

"C'mon, guys, back inside." They fed the puppies, and got them settled back in their area, and Nolan reached again for Harrison's hand. He wasn't nervous—at least, he didn't look nervous, but this was a big moment for him. It had to be. "Want to see my room?"

"Yeah," Harrison answered with a rasp, and squeezed his hand.

They walked down the small hallway, and Nolan pointed out Diego's bedroom before they stepped into his own. It was a little bigger, and Nolan had his own bathroom, and even though it was just the two of them for the next few hours, Nolan closed the door and turned on a small lamp. "Let me give you the grand tour. Bed, bathroom, closet. Office," he added, and pointed at a desk with his laptop and some notebooks with his business ideas.

Harrison looked around, and when Nolan sat on the bed, he followed. "You wanna talk first, or just—" Nolan kissed his cheek again. "Do some of that?"

"I want more of that, yeah. I want to make you feel good." Harrison swallowed. "Will you show me?"

Nolan nodded and leaned forward to kiss him again. His hand reached up and pulled at the buttons of Harrison's shirt, and once it opened, Nolan reached in and touched that pelt of chest hair, soft and thick.

Harrison swallowed as Nolan stroked his chest. "That feels so good," he whispered.

Nolan tugged the shirt off Harrison's broad shoulders. "This is—" Nolan's fingers stroked Harrison's pectoral muscles and strong biceps, watching them flex under his touch. "You're so fucking sexy, Harry, and you keep it all covered up, hidden away from the world."

Harrison smiled and ducked his head. "I'm glad you like it."

"Honestly, if I'd known you were such a snack, I'd never have let you go to the club." Nolan's thumb grazed a pert nipple , his eyes going wide when Harrison shivered at that touch. "What if someone else discovered this before me?"

"That wouldn't have happened. I was there for you." Harrison reached for Nolan, who stood in front of him to make it easier. Nolan's fingers played with Harrison's soft hair as he pulled off Nolan's sweater. Harrison looked up and caught Nolan's eyes, as unsteady hands unbuttoned Nolan's pants. "More?"

"Yes please." One deep breath, and Harrison unzipped Nolan's pants, tugging them down toward his knee. That momentary hesitation twisted Nolan's heart.

This was more than just sex, and they both knew it.

Nolan kicked off his shoes and reached out to steady himself on Harrison's shoulder as he pulled his pants the rest of the way off. He stood only in his black, form-fitting underwear for a second before he climbed back on the bed and straddled Harrison again , those strong arms wrapping tight around him just like the night before in his car.

But this time, they were alone on Nolan's bed, just the two of them.

Nolan cupped Harrison's cheeks, the stubble rough under his fingers, and Harrison looked up at Nolan, eyes wide and open and happy. "Tell me what you want."

"I want you to touch me. And—" Harrison tipped his face up and Nolan kissed him. "I want to see you come."

Nolan pressed his forehead against Harrison's. "We can do that." Touching, yes, Nolan wanted to touch this man, and wanted Harrison to touch him. But first—"Let's get you more comfortable."

After Nolan climbed off Harrison, he shifted toward the back of his bed and pulled Harrison with him. "Shoes off." Nolan's fingers worked at Harrison's belt and the buttons on his pants. It took a minute and some playful fumbling until he was in his boxer-briefs. "You find these comfy?" Nolan asked and tugged at the waistband.

There was that smile again. "I like the coverage." Harrison leaned back on the bed and pulled Nolan on top of him, and Nolan's hands explored Harrison's body while he ran his hands through Nolan's soft chestnut waves. "But I think I'll be more comfortable without them."

"Yeah, that sounds good." Nolan shifted off to kneel next to Harrison and tugged at his underwear, inch by inch. Harrison's stiff cock bobbed out as the thin cloth slid down his thighs and off his legs. "Wow."

Thick and solid, his cock head leaked with precum. Nolan's hand grasped Harrison's cock, his thumb rubbing the sticky slick over his skin. Then Nolan lifted his thumb to his mouth. Harrison's eyes went wide as he pulled Nolan down to him, and then they kissed again , Harrison's tongue plunging deep into Nolan's mouth, chasing that taste.

Nolan reached down and pulled Harrison's hand to his cock, next to his own. "Show me what you like." Harrison gripped his shaft and tugged it, long, slow strokes from base to tip. Nolan followed with his own hand, matching stroke for stroke. "Like this?" he asked, mesmerized by the sights of their hands.

"Yeah," Harrison said, his voice raw and husky . He flushed down through his chest, naked and hard and needy in Nolan's bed. "And you? I wanna touch you."

Nolan groaned and put Harrison's hand on his shaft. "This, yeah, right here. It's super sensitive." Any sensations right around Nolan's cock head sent him flying, and Harrison's fingers circled around his dick and squeezed. "Oh God, yes." He reached over into the table next to his bed and pulled out some lube, and after dribbling some on their fingers, he went back to jerking Harrison off. Their legs tangled awkwardly, but soon they found that sweet rhythm, settling against each other, and the room filled with the sound of their loud breathing, panting into each other's mouths.

Nolan's fingers explored between Harrison's legs, and when Nolan squeezed that heavy sac, Harrison groaned. "I'm close."

"Me too." Nolan stroked him again and found that rhythm that Harrison liked. Harrison's hips thrust up into Nolan's fist and then his back arched and he stilled, pulsing out over Nolan's fingers. "Oh God..."

Nolan leaned over and kissed him, Harrison's pupils blown and dark and focused on Nolan. "Lay back," Harrison murmured, and rolled onto his side, gripping

Nolan's cock tighter. Nolan gasped, grasping Harrison's hip as he continued those short, rough strokes Nolan had shown him, and less than a minute later, he let out a whine and came all over Harrison's hand.

It took a minute to catch their breath, and Nolan reached down and grabbed his underwear, handing them to Harrison to clean up. "That was good."

Harrison's laugh was like a bark. "That was amazing." He kissed Nolan's shoulder, his chin, and his mouth. "What's that on your ass?"

Nolan groaned, embarrassed. "I lost a bet." Shifting onto his side, Nolan bit his lip and shook his head. "If you never want to see me again, I'll understand."

Harrison laughed again, the sweetest sound in the world. "It can't be that bad."

Nolan rolled onto his stomach, and Harrison bent his head to get a better look.

I like my butt

and I cannot lie

Harrison let out a loud exhale. "I stand corrected. That's awful."

Nolan picked up a pillow and hit him with it, and both of them laughed until they couldn't breathe.

Harrison dropped a soft kiss on Nolan's butt tattoo and then sat up. "I should probably go now."

Nolan understood. Living with a roommate wasn't ideal for overnight guests, especially when he hadn't told Diego that he would have overnight company.

Even worse, when Nolan hadn't told him he was dating Diego's lawyer.

"Thank you for taking me out tonight." They collected Harrison's clothes and put them back on, sneaking kisses and touches as he dressed. "I'll talk to you soon?"

Harrison finished buttoning his shirt and slipped on his shoes. "Definitely." Nolan pulled the sweater back on and walked Harrison to the door, and after one more searing kiss, they said goodnight and he left.

Wow. Of all the things Nolan had imagined doing with Harrison that night, laying in his bed and jerking each other off hadn't been at the top, and yet—it made perfect sense, and had been more emotional than other experiences he'd had with other guys, even when they'd gone further sexually.

But now Nolan yawned and stretched. He let the dogs out of their gated area for some play time and was heading back to his room when the front door opened again. "Hey there." Nolan nodded at Diego, who didn't smile back. "You work late tonight?" he asked, concerned about Diego's mood. "Everything okay?"

"I got off an hour ago. But I saw you had a special guest, and I didn't want to interrupt you two."

Fuck. "Look, I meant to tell you—"

Diego stopped walking toward his bedroom and wheeled around to face Nolan . "Tell me what, that you're fucking my lawyer?"

"We're not—I mean, we just had dinner and hung out. I'm sorry," Nolan added when Diego walked off down the hall toward his room. "I should have said something to you."

"Yeah, you should have. I'm hearing all this from everyone else—you and Troy's dad hooking up at Delirium last night, and then I come home tonight and see his car in the parking lot."

When Diego brought up Troy, Nolan's stomach lurched. *I jerked off Troy's dad.* "You want me to stop seeing him?"

Diego sat on his bed. "I don't know."

Nolan sat down on the floor. Bandit crawled into his lap, and he stroked that silky fur. "What are you worried about?"

Diego shrugged, his face dark with anger. "I don't want my lawyer to get dicked around and decide to fuck up my case because you hurt his feelings. That's the first thing that comes to my mind."

"I'm not dicking around with him." Nolan waited until Diego looked at him, eye to eye, before he continued. "I really like this guy."

Smokey joined them and headed for Diego's bed. Diego reached down and put the puppy next to him. "You know, Troy's so pissed about this. Noah told him last night that his dad was over at Delirium, and he thought it was a big joke, until someone showed him a picture of you two dancing or something."

Oh shit. Harrison was going to hear an earful from his son, no doubt. "No matter what happens, he wouldn't fuck up your case because he was mad at me. He's not that kind of man. But if you want us to cool it until the case is over—"

Diego exhaled and his shoulders slumped forward. "You guys... just be careful, okay? Even before this, Troy was worried about his dad. He just got divorced and all. And you, Nolan, I don't ever remember you going out with anyone that much older than you. It's different, you know. You're from entirely different places in your life."

"Yeah, I know. And this is just starting out. It might not go anywhere, and we might just end up good friends." Even as Nolan spoke the words, he knew they weren't true. What he felt for Harrison wasn't like anything else he'd felt in a long time. Maybe ever.

Was it too soon to think that Harrison might be the one?

But Diego didn't need to hear this right now. "I'll talk to him. And—" Nolan bit his lip and sighed. "I'll talk to Troy. I don't want him to think this is just me being my normal stupid."

Diego didn't quite look relieved, but they'd reached an impasse and that was enough for tonight. "Okay. I'm jumping in the shower now." He put the puppy on the floor and frowned. "Wait... Is that my new sweater? Are you wearing my brand-new sweater?"

Oops.

Chapter 14

Harrison's phone alarm went off early the next morning, but he hit the off button and crashed back into his pillow. No early morning trip to the gym today. He'd had vivid dreams filled with Nolan and those talented hands touching him, how Nolan tasted when they kissed.

Harrison's morning erection was rock hard and needed satisfying.

The sky had been drizzling all morning, threatening to derail his plans for working on the yard, but by lunchtime the sun was out, and it had turned into a beautiful spring day. After Harrison reviewed his swimming pool supplies from last year, he drove to the hardware store and picked up the pool chemicals he needed.

Harrison had just taken off the cover and was clearing the drains when the back door to the house opened and closed, and Troy waved from the deck. Harrison beckoned him over and grinned. "Hey kid. I wasn't expecting you."

"Hi Dad." Troy walked over and gave Harrison a hug. "That time again?"

Harrison nodded. "It'll be warm soon, and I enjoy swimming. And I know you and your friends like to come over and use the pool." But Troy's face hardened at those words, and Harrison understood why he was here. "Want some lunch?"

"Maybe. I'm not hungry right now." Troy folded his hands. "I wanted to talk to you about some stuff I heard."

Yep, this was going to be bad. "Okay." Harrison put the pool chemicals down, and sat on one of the patio chairs, quiet as Troy settled next to him. Harrison's stomach churned. "So, what have you heard?" he asked and tried to keep his voice even.

Troy took a deep breath. "I don't even know where to begin. What's going on with you?" He paused, then caught Harrison's eyes. "Are you gay?" he asked.

Here it was. Harrison's fingers tapped against his leg as he sought the right way to explain. "I don't know what's going on, Troy. I like men and women. And I always have." The words slipped out, and once he started talking, it was easier than Harrison expected. "And—I don't know what that makes me. But it's not new, these feelings I have. I just never acted on it before. It was something that I kept private and didn't share."

Troy's face didn't change as Harrison spoke, and he worried Troy was upset with him. "Did Mom know?"

Harrison hesitated. "She knew a little. I don't want to talk about her. What she knew or didn't know—that's between us."

Troy folded his arms and stared. "This isn't why you split up? Because you like guys too?"

What? "No—at least, I don't think so." But upon reflection, how much of that was true? "Your mom wasn't happy with our marriage and wanted to find someone who would make her happy. That had nothing to do with—with any of this."

Troy sighed.

Harrison stood. "Let's go inside and get a drink." Troy followed Harrison into the house, and after grabbing some cold soft drinks from the fridge, they sat on the barstools next to the kitchen island. "For the record, I didn't look for this. I wasn't planning on 'coming out' or anything like that. It just... happened."

"You and Nolan?"

Harrison nodded.

Troy scrubbed his face with his hand. "It's just a lot all at once, Dad. First, I find out that you're out dancing at a gay club with some of my friends. I'm thinking, okay, maybe he's just having fun, meeting new people. But it's not just that, is it? Are you dating him?"

"I don't know," Harrison said with a small shrug. "We went out for dinner and walked around Buffalo Bayou and talked. I like spending time with him."

"But people saw you."

That hurt. "Are you worried people would find out I like guys, too?"

Troy's fingers fidgeted on the table. "A little, yeah. And I'm worried that you might get serious too fast, that this is some sort of infatuation, and you might get hurt. What happens at work when they find out?"

"I get that you're upset, but I'm not a kid, Troy. First, this isn't serious, at least not yet." Troy's eyes widened at that, but Harrison continued. "I like Nolan. I like him a lot. He makes me feel—" Cherished. Sexy. Desirable. "He makes me feel good about myself again, and I enjoy being around him."

Troy frowned. "He's three years older than me, Dad."

"Yeah..." Harrison shook his head, that statement like a punch to his gut. "I didn't look for this. It just happened, and I know what it looks like."

"Did he come on to you?"

"No. I mean—" *So that's what Troy thought.* "Nolan's not that kind of guy. There were a few occasions where we had the opportunity to talk to each other on a personal level, and we became friends. He opened up to me about his life, and I told him about mine." He drifted into professional legal speech, as if that made it easier to explain. "The attraction was mutual, and we agreed to act on it."

Troy's face darkened again. "What about Diego's case?"

Harrison scoffed. "None of this is going to affect the lawsuit."

"Are you even allowed to date someone involved in the case?"

"I'm not breaking any laws," Harrison answered.

But Troy wasn't satisfied. "But it's not completely on the up and up, is it?"

Harrison took another sip from his soft drink. "I'll feel better about all of this once the case is over."

Troy sighed. "So, what you're saying is that you plan on seeing him again?"

"Yeah, if he's interested." Nolan's face floated in Harrison's head, his kisses and his smile. But what if it had just been a bit of fun for him? Just another weekend fling? "We haven't talked about it yet." Troy looked down at his hands, his brows still furrowed. "Are you mad?"

Troy's shoulders slumped. "Mad? I don't know. I'm confused as fuck, Dad. A year ago, you and Mom were sitting here in the kitchen, eating your breakfast together like normal parents, and everything was good. Now she's living uptown with her tennis instructor and you're dating someone my age. A guy my age. Yeah, it's a lot to process."

Troy's downcast expression hurt Harrison's heart, but Troy was right. It had been selfish of Harrison, as a parent, to not consider Troy's feelings in all of this. He'd been so wrapped up in his wants and desires that he hadn't reasoned how it affected his son. "I wanted to talk to you about it. I guess I just didn't think it would get back to you so soon." After a moment's silence, Harrison reached for Troy's arm. "I'm sorry if this hurts you."

Troy didn't pull away, but his soft voice wavered. "I'm worried more than anything. I know you're a grown up, but I don't think you've been in a good mental place since

Mom left. You're a successful guy with money in the bank, and I had expected a few gold diggers to crawl out of the woodwork and try to turn your head their way. I just hadn't expected it to be—"

Harrison sat upright in his chair. "You think he's after my money?" He scoffed and shook his head. "I'm not made of gold, Troy. This isn't a fortune."

Troy rolled his eyes. "It's a lot, Dad, and if I didn't know Nolan, I'd worry about you being taken advantage of by someone half your age looking to make a quick buck."

"Nolan's a good guy."

Troy nodded. "He is... and that worries me as well. What if this gets serious?"

Harrison's heart ticked faster at that thought. "What if it did?"

"This just—it isn't like you. New haircut, you got the five o'clock shadow thing going. Dancing at gay clubs in Montrose..." Troy shook his head again.

"But it is me." Harrison squeezed his hand. "I haven't felt this good in years. I like Nolan, and I think he likes me. And even if it doesn't go anywhere, I'm grateful that he showed me a world out there where I can be who I am without shame."

Troy peered into Harrison's face, searching for something. When Harrison smiled, Troy smiled back, satisfied. "Okay."

They'd gotten over the worst of it, or so Harrison assumed. Then Troy asked, "Does Mom know who you're dating?"

That was it, the last straw, and Harrison snapped. "It's none of her business, is it?" Troy blinked, and Harrison sighed. "I've tried hard this whole time to keep my feelings about your mom out of our relationship. But she left me, Troy. She left and I don't feel like any part of my life is her concern anymore. And I'd appreciate it if you didn't talk to her about it."

Troy bit his lip and dropped his eyes, and Harrison realized then that they'd already discussed it. "Yeah, okay," he said.

Oh, what a mess. "How about I order a pizza, and you come outside and help me with the pool?"

"Yeah, of course." Troy leaned over and they hugged. While Troy didn't quite understand everything—hell, Harrison didn't understand it either—it seemed Troy trusted him enough to find what he needed on his own.

Chapter 15

Saturday was always the busiest day at the salon, so Nolan took Sunday and Monday off as his 'weekend.' On Sundays, his mother often made a big family lunch for her sons, as well as any of their friends who could make it. Nolan cherished those lunches as he grew older and saw his family less frequently. He enjoyed the time they spent together as a family. Even though Noah drove him nuts sometimes, Nolan loved his twin brother a lot.

But on the day after his first date with Harrison, Nolan sent his mom a text and told her he couldn't make it for lunch. Headache, Nolan pleaded as an excuse—but that wasn't the real reason.

He just didn't want to deal with Noah today, especially in front of their mother or any of her friends. Nolan wasn't ashamed of what happened, but he also wasn't ready to discuss it.

Instead, Nolan tackled the mountain of laundry that had piled up inside his closet and caught up on a Netflix series that everyone at work wanted his opinion on (it was great). Even though Nolan hadn't heard from Harrison all day, he also didn't text him. No hurry, no rush in whatever was happening between them.

They both needed a day to breathe and assess where they were and what they were thinking.

But around seven that evening, Nolan's phone pinged. It was a message from Noah—just a photograph of the barbecue grill on his patio with a giant foiled-wrapped chunk of meat on it.

Fuck.

Most families in Texas have a grill master, one person who takes pride in lovingly tending the barbecue, making sure the meat ended up tender and juicy, instead of dry and stringy.

For the Reynolds clan, that person was Noah.

From early on, he developed a knack for barbecuing meats and veggies out on a grill, could debate the finer points of charcoal versus propane, and each Thanksgiving cooked the most mouthwatering smoked turkey Nolan ever tasted—and Nolan hated turkey. Cooking in general wasn't something Nolan cared about, but when they were younger, the twins spent long hours outside, looking up at the stars and talking about their dreams as Noah slow-roasted a brisket overnight.

This text message—it wasn't just Noah's way of saying he wanted some brisket sandwiches for the week. This was an invitation to come talk, maybe even a peace offering.

Nolan had to go.

Twenty minutes later, the harnessed dogs were in the backseat of Nolan's car, along with some clothes for the next day and his contact lens solution. Nolan sent a text to Diego and told him he and the dogs would be at his brother's house for the night.

Noah was a proper grown-up and had a proper house south of downtown Houston, about twenty minutes from where Nolan lived and close to the university where he taught history classes. He must've been standing at the window waiting, because the front door opened as Nolan pulled up into his driveway. "How big?" he asked and opened the back door to let the puppies out.

"Fourteen pounds." Noah grabbed the dogs' leashes from Nolan, and they all walked into the house. "You'll be able to take some home if you stick around."

"Best offer I've had all day." After Nolan dropped his backpack on the sofa, he noticed the empty space in the kitchen where cabinets should go, ripped up holes in the drywall. Nolan would ask about that later. Noah had walked past the kitchen and into the backyard, so Nolan followed, Smokey and Bandit on his heels.

After Nolan unleashed the puppies, they took off, running around Noah's small backyard, sniffing everything they could find. Noah dropped onto a chair next to his round patio table. But Nolan kept walking and stopped in front of Noah's most prized possession—a combination grill smoker. "Why did you get one so big?" Nolan asked and poked the foil-wrapped meat. "That's a lot of meat, even if you give some to me."

Noah shrugged. "It was the prettiest slab they had. And —I haven't done one of these in a while."

"It looks good." Nolan closed the grill lid and sat down in a patio chair next to his brother. Noah leaned over and reached into the mini fridge he kept on the patio, always stocked full of Lone Star beer. He pulled out two and handed one to Nolan, who sighed, pulled off the bottlecap, and took a long pull with a grimace. "This is awful. I don't know how you drink this every night."

Noah chuckled low. "It's not every night, and you don't have to drink it, you know. I think you left some of that fruity shit you like inside the big fridge."

Nolan shook his head. "It's tradition." From their first early forays into brisket smoking, they drank skunky beer and talked about their plans for the future—two Texas boys with big dreams. "This stuff is okay," Nolan said, and choked it down theatrically.

Noah snorted. "Suit yourself."

Nolan set his beer down on the table next to a closed laptop and a thick book, something historical from the look of the cover. "How are your classes going?"

"Teaching or taking?" Noah asked with a cheeky grin.

Show-off. Nolan rolled his eyes. "Either. Both."

Noah nodded. "Teaching is good. I swear the freshmen are stupider each year that I do this. I actually had a student this semester whose mom emailed me to explain why he was late on his discussion posts and could I pretty-please give him more time to finish his work."

Nolan burst out laughing. "You're kidding. I can't imagine asking Mom to do that." Nolan pictured it in his head for a moment, then asked, "How about your classes for your grad school program?"

"Good, great really." Noah dangled his beer bottle in front of him before he spoke, a nervous tell. "I think I've got my dissertation topic nailed down, and maybe even my committee set up. Just waiting for them to email me back."

Nolan understood enough about the PhD process to know that was a big deal. "That's exciting. What are you thinking?"

"Origins of the modern social classes and their effect on politics in pre-revolutionary Russia." Noah exhaled and grinned nervously. "Let's see how it goes."

Nolan made a strangled sound. The social what? "That sounds absolutely awful, but you'll be great." Noah was born with the brains in the family. He always figured out the right way to do things, he always made the right choices and got the results he wanted, every time. But Noah worked hard for what he wanted, so Nolan couldn't begrudge his twin any of his successes. Instead, Nolan raised his bottle. "I'm proud of you, brother."

Noah laughed. "Thanks. I think I'm on the right path." He took another long drink from his beer, and they watched the puppies chase bugs in the grass. Finally—"So, when are you going to tell me about him?"

Here it was. "Don't guess I have much of a choice, do I?" Nolan drank some more beer and winced.

Noah laughed. "Not really. You can't keep any secrets from me. Besides, who else are you going to talk to about this?"

The worst part was that Noah was right. There was Diego, of course, and a few close friends from work, but Noah and Nolan had always been there for each other. Whatever Nolan told his brother stayed in the vault, and no matter how angry they got, they'd always be there for each other. "We had dinner last night, walked around the park, and then went back to my place."

"Oh, a proper date then." Noah pulled another patio chair close and put his legs up. "Did he pay for dinner?"

The corners of Nolan's mouth tugged up. "Yeah."

Noah nodded. "And he's a proper gentleman, too. Did you fuck him?" Nolan didn't answer, just took another drink and looked away with a roll of his eyes. "Okay, so not yet. That means you're either playing hard to get, which isn't like you—you've put out on the first date before with no qualms whatsoever. Or maybe he wasn't into it, a strong possibility given the circumstances. Or—you really like him, and you're terrified."

The logic to Noah's thought process irritated Nolan, and when he still didn't answer, Noah's eyes widened. "Oh wow, so it's the last one. You really like him."

Nolan's beer bottle slammed down on the table with more force than necessary. "I don't see how any of this is your business," he said.

But Noah took Nolan's tantrum in stride. "Ordinarily, I'd agree with you, and all of this would just be to bust your balls. And that will happen, I promise. But we'll discuss that later. First, I just want to make sure you're okay. You're my brother, and I love you, and I can only imagine what's going on inside your head. Just from looking at you, I can tell you're about to explode. So, talk." Noah finished his beer and pulled out another one. "No bullshit, no judgment. Tell me what's going on and get it off your chest."

Fuck it all, he was right. Good thing it was dark now, and Noah couldn't see him blushing. "We're taking it slow. I know we should wait until after the trial to do anything, but..." Nolan held up his hands in an 'I don't know' gesture. "I've never met anyone like him. On the outside, he's this professional—calm, cool, mature guy. Totally got his shit together. But inside, he's soft, and not in a bad way. He's sweet and curious. Right now everything is new to him, and I enjoy being around him." Nolan fiddled with the bottle cap from his beer. "I like being the one showing him what it's like."

Wait—shit. Nolan shut his mouth immediately, and knew he'd said too much.

Noah's brow arched. "So he hasn't dated many guys?"

Nolan cleared his throat. "I—that's kind of private. I don't want to talk about who or what he's done before."

Noah whistled low. "You are in deep, Nolan. You've never had any problem giving me details about all your past conquests before, even shit that I never, ever, ever wanted to know about your sex life."

But Noah's attempt at levity didn't make Nolan laugh. "He isn't a conquest," he said in a quiet voice. The dogs scrambled over and sat down on the patio next to them, panting heavily. "Harrison's a great guy, but for a myriad of reasons we agreed to take things slow."

Noah got up and went into the house and returned with a bowl of water for the dogs. He studied Nolan's face. "Are you happy?"

Nolan smiled, and this weight lifted off his shoulders. "You know, I am. He's not like anyone else I've ever gone out with before, and I'm not saying that because he's older, though I'm open enough to admit that might have something to do with it. He's kind and considerate. He's curious about me, and not just the flirty, sexy stuff. He thinks I'm interesting. And, yeah, it's nice being with someone who's got his life together, a proper grown-up."

Noah sighed. "Well, that's good. Believe it or not, I'm glad to hear that you're happy, because you deserve someone who cares about you. And I know we give each other shit about our dating lives, but this time, you know there's more at stake than just you and him." Noah leaned forward in his chair. "Diego's worried about how this might affect his lawsuit, more worried than he wants to let on to you. And Troy was just blindsided by all of this and didn't know what to think."

Nolan pinched the bridge of his nose. "How bad is it?"

Noah snorted. "He's not happy. This thing between you two, it came out of nowhere, and his folks, they just split up in the last year, so he's not as comfortable with the whole divorced parents thing as we are." Noah leveled a steady glance at him. "You need to talk to him, and soon. And then there's Mom—"

Woah. "You haven't said anything to her, have you?" Nolan asked and sat straight up. "Please tell me—"

Noah shook his head. "Of course not. But do you want her to hear about it from someone else?"

Fuck, Noah was right. "Once the trial is over and if we decide we want to... pursue this, I'll tell her." It was only a couple more weeks. No more than a month. "You think she'll be mad?"

Noah furrowed his brow and took another long pull from his beer. "Is he older than she is?"

Nolan did a quick calculation in his head. "No, but not by much," Nolan admitted.

"She's going to be concerned, at the very least." Noah nudged Nolan's leg with his foot. "This isn't a sugar daddy situation, is it?"

"What? No, fuck no. I don't want or need anything like that from him." A terrible thought raced through his head.

"Do you think that's what Troy thinks?"

Noah rolled his eyes. "I'm sure it's crossed his mind. Wouldn't you think the same if some kid our age said he wanted to go out with Mom?"

Nolan growled and scrubbed his head with his hands. "I need to talk to Troy."

"Yeah." Noah's timer went off and he got up to check the grill. "Alright, got the temperature perfect, and now it's just gotta sit and deliciously marinate in its own fat." When he settled back in his chair, he turned and faced Nolan again. "So, now that the big stuff is out of the way, tell me what else is going on."

"Not much, just waiting for that trial to be over. Me and Diego, we'll both be glad when it's done. But what about you? What's going on in the kitchen?"

Noah's face went dark. "Same shit. This place is a dump and everything's falling apart. Anyway, the new cabinets should be installed next week."

Now it was Nolan's turn to laugh. "You paid pennies for a fixer-upper and then complain that it needs fixing." He paused and finished his beer. "How's Martin? Is he helping with the renovations?"

Noah waved a hand around. "He's okay. Gets on my damn nerves sometimes, but he's fun for a day or two."

Nolan used to be okay with that. Fun for a couple days. But now he wanted more. "Don't you ever think about settling down one day?"

It was a long moment before Noah spoke. "Do you think people like us can be happy in a relationship?"

Nolan blinked. "You mean gay people?" When Noah nodded, Nolan continued. "I hope so. I don't want to spend the next thirty years just hooking up for fun." Noah's dark expression worried him. "What about you? Don't you want to settle down one day?"

"I guess." Noah messed with the wrapper of his beer bottle and didn't look like he believed that. "You ready to say goodbye to these guys?" he said and glanced down at the dogs sleeping at their feet.

The change of subject didn't surprise Nolan. "Yeah, I guess." Reaching down, he scratched Smokey's back. "I hope they get to stay together. Brothers and all."

Noah looked back up and held out his beer. "To brothers."

Nolan touched his bottle with Noah's, and they cheered the puppies. "To brothers."

Chapter 16

O n Thursday morning, Harrison's phone pinged while he jogged on the treadmill. It was Nolan. Most days, he'd send something around eight, but this was early for him.

Good morning, handsome! I think you said you had court this week. Go get'em, killer. lol.

A GIF of a drag queen dressed up as Judge Judy banging a gavel accompanied this.

They hadn't spoken since Harrison left Nolan's apartment on Saturday night, but they sent a few text messages to each other most days. The insecure part of Harrison's subconscious worried about the lack of talking, but he also understood that Nolan wasn't big on phone calls and had a busy life. When they'd parted, Nolan had left the ball entirely in Harrison's court whether this relationship was something he wanted to pursue.

Harrison texted back a smiley face and a heart and decided to call him later that day and see if he had any weekend plans.

Judge Anderson had strict rules in his courtroom, the first being 'no mobile devices of any kind.' Once their team settled in at the defendant's table, Harrison turned off his phone and slipped it into his pocket, then opened his old leather briefcase while Jania Chin, one of the junior lawyers at the firm, opened up her laptop. "Think this will be over today?" she asked and looked over as Harrison pulled out a thick stack of paper files, organizing them in a straight line.

"Yes." Harrison snorted at the way she eyed his handwritten notes. "I'm pretty confident that the plaintiff's firm has thrown everything they have at us. All their evidence is circumstantial, and we've laid out enough doubt that there were several people who had access to those investment accounts. Any one of their employees could have tampered with them and taken the money."

Jania smiled. "I agree."

A thought struck him. "Why don't you give the closing summation today?"

She blinked. "Are you sure, Mr. Crawford?"

"Yeah. It'll be wonderful experience for you, and I think you can summarize the technical jargon better than I can." Harrison turned to an older gentleman seated next to them. "That is, if you don't mind, Mr. Lomeli?"

"Whatever you think is best, Mr. Crawford." Adam Lomeli smiled at Jania. "I just hope it will be over soon."

The trial ended that day, with their client exonerated of all charges. Jania did an excellent job taking the reins of the last day, the jury drawn into her quiet yet confident tones. "Let me take you both out for a beer," Adam Lomeli said after he thanked them. But Jania had to run to the courthouse and submit a brief for another case before the end of the day.

"These kids, the way they hustle, all that energy. We were like that once, you remember?" Adam Lomeli said with a laugh as she jogged down the street and into another building. "Guess that leaves just us."

"Sounds good. Let me check in first." Harrison turned his phone back on—and wished he hadn't. With a deep sigh,

Harrison shook his head. "Looks like I'm going to have to take a raincheck on that beer."

It was a text from Alicia. *She's here.*

Harrison's stomach tightened as he stood in the elevator, heading up to his office. Each step only brought more questions, even though he knew the answer to all of them.

Nolan.

Alicia stood guard in the lobby area, hands on her hips and her eyes flashing dark with anger. "She insisted on waiting in your office. I couldn't stop her."

"That's fine. Probably better that she's off in there where she can't make a scene." Harrison's divorce from Jenny hadn't been publicly contentious, but his colleagues, and Alicia in particular, knew what it had taken out of him, and what Harrison had sacrificed to make sure things stayed outwardly pleasant. "Hold my calls until she's gone."

Jenny stood behind his desk, her dress as red as a fire truck, looking at the photographs of their family that he'd kept on the credenza behind him. Even though she'd heard Harrison enter, she didn't turn around and wouldn't until he addressed her. The bottle of bourbon that he kept in the bottom drawer was on top of the desk—of course she'd made herself at home. "What do you want?" he asked and closed the office door behind him.

She turned, holding a glass with a generous pour of liquor. Her long fingernails were the same color as her dress. "Answers, mostly. And maybe a little something extra."

Harrison snorted. "Blackmail wasn't ever your game." He walked to his desk and sat down, forcing her to the other side. "You can't be out of money yet."

She seated herself and sipped from her glass while she took in Harrison's appearance, looking down her sharp nose at him. "I heard some things from Troy and wanted to find out straight from the old horse's mouth—just so I know what to say when our friends ask."

"You can just ask if you're curious. There's no need for any sort of excuse." Harrison tucked the bottle back into the bottom drawer and made a mental note to get a lock installed on his desk. "I went out on a dinner date with a charming young man."

"He's your son's age."

"I'm aware of how old Nolan is." A thought crossed his mind. "Does that bother you more than the gay part?"

Jenny's nose wrinkled, as if deep in thought. "It might. Isn't that peculiar?" She laughed. "I almost said, 'Isn't that queer?' but that's a different conversation, isn't it?" Her expression softened. "What's going on with you?"

Harrison had nothing to hide, so he went with the truth. "I don't know. It isn't something I went out looking for, but —" He shrugged. "It happened, and it's exciting."

She tilted her head. "Are you happy?" For a moment Harrison wondered if maybe she really wanted to talk like friends, like two people who'd known each other intimately for twenty-five years.

He smiled. "I am. He makes me feel—"

"Young?" she asked.

Harrison shook his head. "I don't want to feel young. I want to feel attractive. Wanted. Sexy, even. And... he likes me." He pointed at Jenny and back at himself. "You and me, we haven't liked each other in a long time. And that wasn't all your fault."

His honesty surprised her; he could see it. "This will ruin your career."

Harrison didn't think it would, but there was no sense in arguing with her about that. "Wasn't much of a career if my choice of romantic partner can derail it."

That hit a nerve. His lack of concern. "Don't you care what happens to you? To everything that you worked your whole life to build?"

"Honestly? No." Harrison held up his hand and counted on his fingers. "Troy is grown. You're gone. It's just me I have to look out for now, and I can live simply. I never needed the big house in the fancy zip code." What Harrison didn't mention (and what she already knew) was that there was more than enough money in the bank to live off if he budgeted right and didn't go crazy with silly expenses.

But Jenny scoffed. "I know it's never been just the money with you. But you didn't buy the fancy house and expensive car just because I wanted them. You always needed the respect of your colleagues, all these men and women who admire you. You needed their respect so much more than you wanted mine. Can you live with all of them turning their backs on you? Deriding your accomplishments? Can you go on here in this town once you become the gay lawyer who used to be a partner at Barton, Simmons, and Crawford?"

She hit her target straight on, but Harrison didn't flinch. "I don't think that will happen."

She snorted and stood, setting her empty glass on his desk. "We'll see about that."

"Weren't you going to try and needle something out of me?" It was better if he knew what damage she sought to inflict.

"I thought about it, but—" Jenny clasped her purse in front of her. "It might be more fun to watch you walk along this tightrope and figure it all out yourself. Just—don't hurt our son." Her eyes flashed with anger. "He's been through a lot already."

It was on the tip of his tongue to mention that their family drama had been instigated by her leaving their marriage for her tennis instructor, but Harrison didn't want to fight. None of this mattered.

But he couldn't resist one last comment. "Give Bill my regards."

Her face froze a moment, then she turned and left without looking back.

A quick glance at Harrison's desk told him she had found nothing that might have been used to incriminate him, but he'd secure the office better in the future, just in case. Harrison reached for the family picture on his credenza and set it in his briefcase. There were other photographs at home, ones with just him and Troy. He would replace this one with any of those, or maybe even take some recent pictures with his son the next time they got together.

It was after five, and Harrison wanted to leave, but there was one last item on his to-do list.

Hey hon. Last day of court, and we won. :) I hope you had a good day too.

Want to come to my house this weekend? I can make you dinner after you get off work on Saturday.

You can stay as long as you want.

Harrison hit SEND before he chickened out and deleted the last sentence.

The reply came just as he got to his car.

I'd love to. See you then. [heart emoji]

Chapter 17

"Okay guys, I'm off to work now, and I'll be back sometime tomorrow afternoon. Promise me you'll be good boys for Diego, and on your best behavior." Nolan slung an overnight bag over his shoulder, packed with clothes for the next day, his swim trunks, and contact lens supplies. The puppies, playing on the floor of his bedroom, stopped chewing on each other's tails long enough to look up at him and tilted their heads. "I know I can count on you."

Behind him, Diego stood in the doorway and snorted. "We've got a good weekend planned, don't we, guys? I've got the whole day off, and the new Planet Zombie game is dropping at two. We're gonna order pizza and destroy the undead on the Xbox all night. My sister might stop by and hang out with me. It's been a while since we've hung out."

Nolan liked Diana, and he'd miss seeing her. "Tell her she can stay in my room if she wants to spend the night." He bit his lip, deep in thought. "Pretty sure there's nothing lying around that would scare her."

Diego burst out laughing. "I'll let her know." Then Nolan caught his roommate's eyes, dark and worried. "And you have a good time tonight too." This was hard for Diego, and he'd continue to worry about what was happening between Nolan and Harrison, at least until they settled this stupid lawsuit.

That guilt itched at Nolan's conscience, but the desire to be with Harrison overwhelmed him. "Thanks, man. I'm sure I will." Each dog got a quick scratch behind the ears. "See you all tomorrow."

The salon was packed, even for a Saturday. Customers bustled in and out of Nolan's chair all day long, and more than one client inquired about the sparkle in his gray eyes and the cheeky grin on his face. Even Enrique pulled him aside during their lunch break and wanted to know what was up.

"I've got a hot date tonight," was as much as Nolan shared with anyone.

But it bothered him, not being open and honest with his friends. Until the situation was more settled with Harrison, the smart move was to keep it all under wraps.

When Angel told Nolan that his last scheduled client of the day moved his appointment to the following week, Nolan almost hooted in delight—he could leave work an hour earlier than planned. After he sent a quick text to Harrison, Nolan jumped in his car and sped toward Harrison's house. But the closer Nolan got, the more this nervous energy bubbled inside him, especially as he pulled off the highway and into the neighborhood where Harrison lived.

Tree-lined streets with luxurious houses and expensive cars parked in the driveways were a far cry from Nolan's two-bedroom apartment. Of course, it made sense now— the idea that Nolan might be interested in Harrison's money.

Finally, Nolan reached Harrison's subdivision and, after entering the gate code, he drove slowly and gawked at the mansions until he found Harrison's street and pulled up toward his house. The exterior of the house was breathtaking, white stone and glass, with a perfectly manicured front yard as large as the house where Nolan grew up. He pulled into the driveway, turned off his car, and sat for a moment to collect his thoughts.

This was a big step for both of them. Nothing would be the same after tonight.

Harrison answered the door in a t-shirt and shorts. Nolan had never seen him dressed this casually, and the sight of Harrison's knobby knees made him grin. "Hey," Harrison said, and kissed Nolan's cheek as he walked in. "I'm glad you made it early."

"Me too." Standing in the entryway, Nolan gasped. The ceiling had to be at least twenty feet high, tile and marble everywhere, and he tried not to stare like some country mouse. "This is huge."

"I told you, it's too much for one person." They walked into the main living room, another enormous room flanked on one side by a huge stone mantle and fireplace. "Over there is the kitchen, and the pantry is through that door." White, clean marble, that was Nolan's first impression of the kitchen, with a large island in the kitchen surrounded by bar stools. "My home office is over there, but I don't use it much." The cold beauty of the house reminded Nolan of houses he'd seen in upscale magazines—pristine and perfect, without warmth or decoration.

A house, but not a home.

Upstairs, Harrison pointed out Troy's old rooms, the guest bedroom, and then led Nolan into his media room. "I spend a lot of time here." Two rows of leather recliners and an enormous flat screen television that took up almost an entire wall. Movie posters hung from the other walls, and it hit Nolan—this was the first room that showed any actual personality, a room that looked like Harrison.

Nolan couldn't keep the delight off his face. "I don't know why you'd ever leave here." Excitement bubbled through him. "Can you imagine hooking this up to a video game system?"

Harrison's arm snaked around his waist. "That sounds like fun. We should try it sometime. Oh, that reminds me, I've got a surprise for you later." Harrison's mischievous smile had Nolan curious, but he didn't press it—just pecked Harrison's cheek with a soft kiss.

It still awed Nolan, all of this. It wasn't an egregious display of wealth, but Nolan's head was certainly turned, his nerves so fixated on the luxury of each room that he didn't realize Harrison had walked them into the master bedroom. A huge glass window looked out over the backyard, with the Houston skyline off in the distance. The room had its own fireplace, across from a huge California King bed.

Harrison shifted against Nolan's side. "Um, you can leave your bag here if you want. I mean, I don't want to assume, and I've got a spare guest room set up if you didn't—"

He's more nervous than I am. Nolan stopped Harrison's words with a kiss. "I'm sure I'll make myself comfortable here." After dropping his bag on the bed, Nolan took Harrison's hands in his, and they looked at each other for a long moment. Standing next to the bed reminded Nolan of what would happen later, and his stomach flipped pleasantly at the thought. But that was later. "You said something about dinner?"

"I did. I've got some steaks marinating, and I thought it would be nice to grill them outside since the weather's so pretty." Harrison's face lit up, and there it was, that smile. "Let me get started on them. Do you want to sit in the jacuzzi while I grill?"

Did he? "Let me grab my trunks."

Harrison's backyard just edged out the media room for Nolan's favorite place in his entire home. The large wooden deck and porch had a covered roof, so it felt almost like an extension of the house and overlooked a perfectly landscaped backyard and kidney-shaped swimming pool. The outdoor kitchen, complete with grill and smoker built into the deck, would have made Noah green with envy.

After Nolan changed into his swimming trunks, he walked to the edge of the swimming pool and dipped his toes; the water felt good. "Maybe we can swim in the morning," What must that be like, to just wake up and head out to his own private pool.

"Absolutely." Harrison set a big plate of meat and cut up vegetables on a table next to the grill as Nolan investigated the jacuzzi. "Let me know if the water's too hot."

Carefully, Nolan stepped into the bubbling water and immediately his muscles relaxed. A loud groan escaped his lips as he sat back against a jet of water. "This is incredible. I would never leave this if I lived here." Nolan instantly regretted his choice of words. After his talk with Noah, any appearance of grasping at Harrison's money had to be avoided.

But Harrison just laughed, and his eyes admired Nolan's body. "We'll see how you feel once you get pruney." He walked over and sat down next to Nolan, dangling his legs in the water. "How do you like your steak?" he asked, and kissed the top of Nolan's head.

"I like it a little pink inside," Nolan said, looking up into Harrison's open and friendly face. "That sounded dirty. I'm sorry. I'm a mess."

But Harrison just laughed again. "You're amazing."

Dinner was another unforgettable experience that showed Nolan a glimpse into Harrison's life. He changed out of his swim trunks into a t-shirt and shorts while Harrison opened a bottle of red wine, and they ate their steaks on the patio as the sky grew dark, and talked about how their days had gone, just like old friends. This might be a typical night for Harrison, just grilling meat and veggies in his backyard, but Nolan appreciated every moment of it.

"That might be the best steak I've ever had. I'm not surprised. I haven't seen you do anything yet that wasn't perfect."

Harrison snorted and dug into his own steak. "You saw me dance the other night. I know I looked like a flailing chicken out there."

Nolan did remember that night. "Nonsense. We looked good."

"Standing next to you helped." Nolan was getting used to those long, lingering glances from Harrison that made his insides swim. "So, what do you think?" Harrison pointed back at the house.

What did Nolan think? "Well, first off, you're right, it's big. Beautiful, but a lot of space for one person. And—" Nolan speared a piece of veg on his fork and held it out in front of him as he spoke. "It doesn't look like you. Everything is elegant and beautiful, but I don't see you. Does that make sense?"

"Perfect sense. And part of me wants to make changes." Harrison shrugged and drank from his wine glass. "Then again, I just don't know how much time and energy I want to spend on changing it if I won't be here much longer."

"What does Troy think?" Harrison's face fell slightly, and Nolan immediately regretted bringing him up. "I'm sorry."

"No, don't apologize. We can't pretend that isn't an issue." Harrison wiped his mouth and sat back, sighing. "I haven't brought up selling the house, but I've mentioned to him it's too big now for just me and I want to make some changes in my life."

"Is one of those changes dating men?" Nolan asked with a wry smile.

Harrison nodded with a snort. "Yeah, we talked about that. I didn't handle any of this the right way, and he's got a right to be upset."

Nolan hoped for Harrison's sake that Troy wasn't angry. "I need to talk to him, too. Maybe later this week, the two of us can chat." Harrison didn't look pleased at that, so Nolan reached for his hand. "He needs to hear it from me, that I am not after your money or looking for some sort of sugar daddy. I like you. I like you a lot, and whatever happens with us, it's because we belong together."

Harrison wasn't convinced, but just nodded. "You mention anything to your mom?"

Nolan's fork fell from his hand, clattering loudly on the plate. "Oh, fuck no, she'll kill me," he whispered. But they both laughed and finished dinner.

Afterward, it took a few minutes to clean up the kitchen. Harrison washed the dishes and wine glasses, and after Nolan dried them, he handed them back to Harrison to put away. The sweet, simple domesticity of it tugged at Nolan's heart. Was this what it was like, sharing your life with a partner? "You said you had a surprise for me?" Nolan asked and watched Harrison pull out a large metal bowl and a bag of popcorn.

The surprise turned out to be a special movie set up in the media room. They curled up next to each other in over-sized recliners as the room went dark. "Wait—is this?"

For the next hour and a half, they ate popcorn and watched Jackie Gleason chase Burt Reynolds and Sally Field across the Deep South toward Atlanta. "This is amazing and awful at the same time," Nolan murmured as the credits rolled across the screen. "I can't believe you rented *Smokey and the Bandit* just for me to watch."

"Oh no. I bought it on DVD for you to keep forever, to remind you of your puppies."

"And tonight." Nolan leaned over and kissed him as a thank you. "It will remind me of tonight, too. Thanks for dinner and this movie and everything." One more kiss, and then another, and soon Harrison's hands wrapped around him and pulled Nolan into his recliner for more delicious kisses .

But it was awkward, the two of them crowded into one seat, and Nolan pulled back reluctantly as nerves hit him. "Um, is there anything you need to do before we turn in?" Nolan asked.

Harrison blinked, and it took him a moment to answer. "Yeah, let me go set the alarm. Do you need anything from the kitchen?"

Nolan bit his lip. "Maybe a bottle of water?"

"I'll be right back." Harrison headed downstairs while Nolan walked into the master bedroom alone. Opening his bag, Nolan grabbed his toothbrush, contact solution, and case, and then set them in the bathroom, which was also large and spectacular, white marble everywhere. Nolan took out his contacts, then looked in the mirror and glared at his blurry reflection. "Don't fuck this up for him." Harrison wasn't a virgin but, in a way, he was, and tonight would be an important first for him.

Nolan couldn't let him down.

By the time Harrison got back to his bedroom, Nolan had settled himself on the bed, turned on a lamp, and caught up on his phone messages. From Harrison's expression, seeing Nolan unsettled him a little. "Are we good?" Nolan asked and set his phone down on the table next to his side of the bed.

Harrison nodded and joined Nolan on the bed, then handed him a bottle of water. "I'm telling myself that even if I were with a woman, after all this time, I'd be nervous, but—"

His hands found Nolan's, and their fingers laced tightly. "Like I said the other night. Nothing's gonna happen that you don't want. But you gotta talk to me, okay?" Nolan reached up and ran his fingers across Harrison's face, the soft scrape of stubble incredibly sexy as Harrison pushed a loose tendril off of Nolan's face. "I can't read minds, and everything works so much better if we communicate."

"I will." Harrison pressed his forehead against Nolan's. Then with a deep sigh, he reached over and pulled out a condom and a small bottle of lube from his nightstand. "Um, what do you like best? How, I mean. How do you like it?" Harrison's emotions sat right on the surface, his eyes dark with worry and need. "I probably should've asked before now."

Time to fix that. Better yet, Nolan decided, they'd fix it together. "Hmm." Nolan laid back down, and tugged Harrison down with him until they faced each other, so close their noses brushed together. "What do I like? I like when I'm on my stomach, and my partner is on top of me, and I can feel all that delicious weight pressing me into the mattress." While Nolan talked, his hand snaked into Harrison's shorts and cupped his semi-hard erection. Harrison's breath caught, but he said nothing as Nolan spoke. "I like being on my back, almost bent in half while my partner is deep inside me, our faces so close we can kiss." Nolan leaned close, and his lips ghosted across Harrison's mouth as he spoke. "I like being the little spoon, a soft, slow fuck from behind." Another kiss, and Nolan pulled his face back to see Harrison's face, his hand still on Harrison's cock, now rock hard and leaking. "Now, you tell me what you want."

Harrison's blue eyes were wide, his pupils blown out. "I want to see your face."

So serious, so beautifully earnest it made Nolan's heart hurt, and nothing was more important right now than getting this right for him. "Okay. Do you trust me, Harry?" Nolan rubbed his thumb over the head of Harrison's cock. He slid the sticky pre-cum over his skin, then Nolan lifted it to his mouth, licking at it with his tongue.

Harrison groaned and touched Nolan's face, then cupped Nolan's cheeks with his hands. "Completely. Tell me what to do."

"First, we've got too many clothes on." Harrison clumsily tugged on Nolan's shirt, and he grinned as Harrison threw it on to the floor, quickly followed by the rest of their clothing. "Now I want you on your back." Nolan straddled Harrison's thighs and handed him the lube. "Two fingers inside me, okay?" Nolan lightly stroked Harrison's thick cock. "You gotta loosen me up for this monster."

It took a minute to position himself so Harrison could reach, but soon those fingers pushed slowly into Nolan, first one and then both. He groaned at the aching stretch. "Like this?" Harrison asked, his voice rough with need , his other hand gripping Nolan's hip.

Nolan dropped his head to kiss him. "Yeah." Pushing back, he fucked himself on Harrison's fingers and made another low sound as he eyed Harrison's cock. "You're gonna feel so good in me."

Harrison's eyes darted between Nolan's face and cock, already leaking a string of precum onto his stomach. "Fuck, I want to taste you so bad."

The idea of Harrison's mouth on Nolan made him groan again. "Soon. If you sucked me right now, I'd blow all over you and I wanna, oh fuck, I wanna wait. Wanna come when you're inside me." They kissed again, and Nolan pulled off Harrison's fingers. "I'm ready."

With shaky hands, Harrison tore the foil wrapper and rolled the thin latex onto his shaft as Nolan settled above him again. One of Nolan's hands joined Harrison's, and together they found that spot, where the blunt head of Harrison's cock pressed against Nolan's wrinkled hole. "Yeah, right there—"

And then Harrison was in him, and Nolan moaned. "Yes..."

Bracing one hand on each of Harrison's shoulders, Nolan slid down his cock, one slow inch at a time until his ass hit skin. "Fuck, Harry..." Harrison's hands gripped Nolan's hips, his entire body strung tight, and Nolan saw how hard it was for him to hold it together.

Nolan raised his ass and lowered it, then again, and watched Harrison's face each time he was balls deep. "Oh fuck, oh fuck…" Harrison murmured those words over and over again, and soon his hips rocked up and into Nolan.

Now it was Nolan's breath that caught in his throat. "Fuck me, baby." Harrison growled, and thrust up again, those hands tight on Nolan's hips as Harrison pumped into him, and they found that sweet rhythm—the slap of Nolan's ass against Harrison's balls, the soft grunts Harrison made with each deep stroke, and the sound of Nolan's breath exhaling each time he got pounded with that thick cock.

Then one of Harrison's hands gripped Nolan's shaft and began to roughly stroke it. Nolan moaned at Harrison intense expression, and it didn't take long for that tug, that heat that pooled inside Nolan's belly. He exploded out all over Harrison's hand and chest with a shout, and his body contracted around Harrison's cock.

A second later, there was a long groan and one deep thrust, and Harrison stilled, his eyes closed tight. Nolan bent his head and kissed Harrison as he caught his breath, Nolan's body still wrapped around him.

Nolan never wanted to leave this. "That was amazing."

Harrison opened his eyes, with all that love and hunger mirrored right back at Nolan. They were dirty and sweaty, cum smeared between their bodies, and yet he pressed the sweetest baby kisses to Nolan's face—his nose, his cheeks, his chin, his eyes , like Nolan was the most precious treasure he'd ever known.

Had he ever felt this cherished after a fuck?

Harrison slipped out of Nolan with a hiss, and he heard the condom fall into a trash basket on Harrison's side of the bed as he stretched out. But then Harrison was back right next to him, those powerful arms tight around Nolan's waist. "Are you okay?" Harrison asked with a tender kiss.

Nolan played with Harrison's chest hair, thick and soft. "I am so good. So fucking good." He glanced down at little Harry, spent and damp between Harrison's legs. "When can I have more?" he asked and batted his eyes.

Harrison laughed, and responded by rolling on top of Nolan, with nothing but kisses and whispered promises between them.

Chapter 18

It was still dark when Harrison woke up the next morning, but he couldn't get back to sleep.

Was it possible to be so happy?

Harrison couldn't recall the last time that sexual intercourse wasn't merely a perfunctory act, making the motions when he or his wife had felt those urges. But just the memory of last night, being with Nolan, *being inside* that tight ass had his heart racing again in a way that his cardiologist definitely not approve. Last night, Harrison learned that sex with a man was, in many way, a lot like sex with a woman. But those small differences—the rough playfulness, and firm, flat planes where before there were curves—delighted him.

Nolan slept next to him, curled up on his side, and his firm, lithe body pressed against Harrison's chest. Last night Harrison had watched in wonder as Nolan's fingers tugged on his chest hair, telling him how sexy it was, how it aroused him.

Unbelievable.

Anything that Nolan wanted, Harrison would gladly give him. All he had to do was ask.

But right now, it was Harrison's body that was asking, his semi-hard cock pressed against Nolan's perfect round ass. Harrison pushed Nolan's hair off of his shoulder and kissed his golden skin. Nolan shifted back against him with a soft groan. "Yes," Nolan whispered, as their legs tangled. "Please."

Please.

Harrison rolled over and opened the nightstand and pulled out another condom, lubing himself up. Just as he was about to press his fingers inside Nolan, he turned his head over his shoulder and gave Harrison a sleepy kiss. "I'm good. Just put it in."

Harrison froze. Maybe he was still dreaming, imaging this beautiful boy in his bed, begging Harrison to fuck him. Harrison's hands spread Nolan's ass cheeks wide as he pushed inside him and looked down. His cock disappeared into that tight asshole and pulled him in deeper and deeper.

The room spun. Harrison closed his eyes and pressed his forehead against the back of Nolan's neck, as he held the younger man close against him. Harrison's arms wrapped around his torso, and they fucked slow and sweet, Nolan's ass rocking back to meet Harrison's thrusts. Everything in his universe focused on the man in his bed, and the way their bodies melded together, so close Harrison couldn't tell where he ended and Nolan began.

Nolan's hand moved to jerk himself off, but Harrison reached for it and held it tight against his side. "Mean," Nolan murmured, but as Harrison's hips picked up speed, he grunted with each thrust, his fists gripping at the sheets. Every nerve ending lit up like a fire, waves upon waves of hunger and need building and rising, and then—a crash, the heat ebbing away, out of him and into Nolan.

Nolan's firm body melted against him, but they weren't finished, not yet.

With one last kiss to his shoulder, Harrison pulled out and took care of the condom. Then he rolled Nolan onto his back and slid down between his legs. "What are you—" was all Nolan got out before Harrison swallowed his cock.

At least, as much as he could. Harrison held onto the base with one hand and sucked on the thick head of Nolan's long, slender cock. He didn't think he would ever take all of it in his mouth, but it would be fun trying, learning what made Nolan happy. "This good?" Harrison asked, learning the taste and feel of another man's cock.

Nolan leaned back on his elbows and watched him. "So good. Fuck, Harry, you're incredible." Nolan's fingers threaded through his hair, and he held Harrison's head steady as he sucked and bobbed his head lower and lower and tried to give him what Harrison thought felt good. With his free hand, Harrison rubbed his thumb against Nolan's wrinkled tender hole, and he felt his body tense up. "Oh fuck."

A minute later, the fingers in Harrison's hair tightened and Nolan groaned, pulling Harrison's head back. "I'm close—" But Harrison held on and when it hit, he swallowed it down, salty and thick, and nosed against Nolan's groin until his softened cock slipped out of his mouth. *So that's what it's like*, Harrison thought.

Nolan's arms pulled Harrison up toward him, and they kissed. "Good morning," Harrison said.

Nolan's smile was like the sun, and his arms wrapped tight around Harrison. "You are full of surprises. Don't tell me that was the first blow job you ever gave. I don't believe you."

A laugh burst out of Harrison. "You know it was." He leaned in and kissed Nolan again. "I just wanted to make you happy."

Nolan's eyes glowed. "That means a lot to me. More than you know." Harrison wanted to understand what that meant, but Nolan sat up, the sheets pooling at his waist. "How about a morning swim before we shower?"

Harrison scratched his head and pretended to think. "Now, did I turn on the swimming pool heater last night? Let me think." When Nolan nudged his shoulder, Harrison laughed. "It should be perfect this morning. I'll make some coffee and meet you out there."

Later that morning, after swimming and caffeine and a shower that got handsy real fast, they settled in for a late breakfast of pancakes and bacon. "So, tell me, counselor," Nolan began, his hair pulled back off his face with a headband as he waved a piece of bacon around in front of him. "How was the experience?"

"Hard to say, Your Honor." Harrison tried to keep from smiling. "I believe I'll need more data to accurately conclude whether or not I enjoyed the activity."

"How much more data?"

Harrison took a bite of the pancakes, his mouth full as he spoke. "Weeks. Months. Maybe years." They chuckled, and then Harrison got serious. "What about you? You had a first timer and an old guy all rolled up into one. Was it as bad as you thought it would be?"

Harrison had expected a flippant answer from Nolan, but to his surprise, Nolan grew thoughtful, too. "The first time I'm with someone, it's often late at night, you know? We've been at a club, dancing, drinking, hooking up. It's exciting and strange and kinda forbidden. At least, that's how it's been for me. But last night, with you—" Nolan set his fork down and folded his hands. "It was like—I had all of those nervous jitters because it was our first time and I wanted to make it good for you, but it also felt like we'd been together for years. Not that it wasn't exciting or amazing, because it was. You were great. Fuck, you were incredible. The sex was outstanding. But the whole time I felt like I was at home with someone who cared about me. Not just someone who wanted *to fuck*, or someone who wanted *a fuck*, didn't matter who it was." He picked up his fork, his face pink as he stabbed a pancake. "That's how you made me feel."

It was a moment before Harrison spoke. "Thank you for saying that."

"I meant it." Nolan grinned, that silly expression on his face. "And also, holy shit, you're hot as fuck." Another smile. "I hope we get together again soon."

"Me too, Nolan."

Me too.

Chapter 19

Harrison wasn't a big texter. Nolan knew this and curbed his expectations after their weekend together. Harrison liked him, cared about him, and that's what mattered, not how much they chatted or texted during the week. But it gave Nolan such a thrill when Harrison sent an unsolicited text in the middle of the day, about something he saw or something he thought.

Nolan loved seeing Harrison's name on his phone screen, even if he didn't like the message.

Change in plans. It looks like Diego's deposition will be Friday and you are scheduled for next Monday. Is that okay?

Nolan hated putting this off even longer, but that worked out better for him. Monday was Nolan's day off, and this way, he didn't have to take off work on Friday, one of his busy days. *Yes, sir. We'll have to spend a long time going over what I need to say. A long, long, LONG time.*

Harrison replied immediately. *I hope so.*

The weekend couldn't come fast enough, but for right now, Nolan had to get back to work. He'd glanced over his bookings for the day, most of them repeat clients who he recognized, but a few newbies as well.

After a quick lunch, Nolan headed to his station and checked in with Angel. "How are we looking?"

"Your one o'clock is here early, if you wanted to get started." She pointed out a woman in the waiting area. "Green dress. Mrs. Crawford."

Same name. *What a coincidence.* But as Nolan walked over to meet her, his smile faded. No, this wasn't a coincidence. Nolan took a deep breath. "Mrs. Crawford?"

She stood, as elegant in her forest green dress as Nolan had imagined she would be, blond hair pulled back off her thin face. She looked him up and down but kept whatever thoughts she had hidden. "Please, call me Jennifer."

"I'm Nolan. Come this way." She followed him to his salon chair and sat down. Nolan's heart pounded like a drum in his chest, but he refused to let it show. "What can I do for you today?" he asked.

"Just a style. I've got dinner with my son this evening, and I wanted to look nice for him."

"No shampoo?"

"No, not this time, thank you."

Whatever else people might describe him as, Nolan prided himself on being, first and foremost, a professional. Staring at her face in the mirror, he inspected her reflection. Her face was a perfect oval, but whoever cut her hair didn't honor that and tried to force long bangs on her. "Is this a formal event? Or do you just want some extra body, some curls up in here."

"No, just dinner at our favorite restaurant." She looked at herself in the mirror. "Curls would be nice. Maybe some height on top."

Nolan draped a cape around her and got to work. After he sectioned her hair, the magic began. "I know you don't have time for anything other than a style today, but have you ever thought about long layers?" Nolan pulled strands off to the side and checked their length. "It would instantly lift everything. You've got some natural bounce in your hair and this straight bob is working against it."

Jennifer looked at herself in the mirror. "I'll consider it. Thank you." She watched in silence as Nolan worked, her eyes never leaving his face. "Troy tells me you have a twin brother."

"I do. He's a professor at the University of Houston." A snort escaped his lips. "He got the brains in the family."

"But that doesn't sound as much fun as what you do. Do you like your job?"

That was a strange question. "I get to meet lots of interesting people, and I go home every day and feel good about making people happy."

Jennifer never took her eyes off him, watching in the reflection. "I heard we have you to thank for Harrison's new hair style ."

There was no crack in Nolan's expression, not one, as he pulled out his curling iron. "I made some suggestions. A little longer on top is very fresh right now."

She laughed. "That's not an adjective I've ever used for Harrison, even when we were young. I used to tease him that he was born an old man."

"I haven't seen that side of him," Nolan said.

"Oh, you will, if you last that long." Nolan frowned as she continued. "I know he's enamored right now, but if he's truly chosen this—lifestyle, I can't imagine that he won't go through a few of you cuties before he gets tired of it all."

"Do you think he's having a mid-life crisis?" Nolan asked and pumped some styling foam into his hand before rubbing it into her fresh curls.

Jennifer chuckled bitterly. "What other explanation do you have? My only hope is that he comes to his senses before he destroys his career." When Nolan's hands stopped, she caught his eye in the mirror's reflection. "You know they'll fire him when it all gets out."

Harrison had assured Nolan that was not the case. This was all designed to get under his skin. He knew that.

But it worked. "Did you just come here to scare me?"

The victory in her eyes infuriated him. "Oh, honey, I was just curious about you. I wanted to see it for myself. But I will say this—you are a magician with hair. Very talented." She turned her face from side to side and admired her reflection. "Long layers. I'll remember that."

After Nolan took off the cape, she walked over to the counter and handed Angel her credit card. "I hope you have a great night with Troy," he said.

"I'm sure we will. Give Harrison my regards," she answered.

Like hell I will. Nolan waited until she walked out of the salon to let go of the breath he'd been holding. The last thing Harrison needed was to find out about this visit of hers.

"Is that who I think it was?" Angel said in a whisper, even though Jennifer was gone.

"Mm-hmm," Nolan nodded. "Girl, can you even..."

Angel leaned against the counter and shook her head. "You and your drama, it never ends. Just like your workday, ha ha. Your next client is here. Carlos Elizondo, blue jean jacket."

That evening, Nolan bit the bullet and called Troy. He wasn't sure if Jennifer Crawford had been truthful about having dinner with him, so he waited until later in the evening when Troy would be home and alone.

The phone rang several times before Troy picked up. "Hey."

Ug. Troy didn't sound excited about talking to him. "Hi. Sorry to call late."

"No problem. What's up?"

Nolan's stomach was in knots. He'd never had this sort of experience before. In his whole life, Nolan had only once dated someone with kids, and that time the child was five years old. "I thought we should talk."

There was a long pause on the other end. Finally— "Yeah. Okay. That's probably a good idea."

He doesn't want to kill me. That's a good start. "Can we get a drink tomorrow? I work until seven. We could meet after that."

"Tomorrow's not good for me. I—" Troy hesitated. "Diego said he wanted to go celebrate Friday when he was done with his deposition. Celebrate or drown his sorrows in Diet Coke, depending on how the day went. I told him I'd go wherever he wanted, and I think he said Delirium. We can talk then if you want."

Nolan wasn't crazy about having a heart to heart with Harrison's son on a Friday night at their local gay club, loud and noisy with other friends around. That also meant that he wouldn't see Harrison that night unless he left right after their talk and headed over to his house.

But Nolan wasn't about to argue with Troy about this. "Sounds good. I'll see you then."

Chapter 20

Friday started off bad and just got worse as the day went on.

First, Harrison hurt himself at the gym—he lost his footing when he stepped off the treadmill, and fell, sprawled on the gym floor. It was more embarrassing than anything else, and he tried to laugh it off. But his ankle ached, and it was sore and painful all morning.

At the office, Alicia clucked around him like a mother hen; she'd already brought in a chair to elevate his foot. "Take this. Samantha had this in her gym bag." She held out an insulated cold pack and placed it gently in Harrison's hands. "Just break it, twist the bag or something, and it will get cold fast. And let me know if you want me to make an appointment with your doctor."

"This will be fine, I promise." Just having the foot elevated lessened the ache. "I've got some of those elastic bandages at home. I'll wrap it up and be good as new tomorrow." Maybe not tonight, though, and the idea of an evening in with Nolan sounded more and more appealing. "At least I won't have to walk much today." Depositions continued for Diego Duarte's case, at long last. The plaintiff had been yesterday, and Diego was set for today. Harrison would spend the day seated next to him. "Has Mr. Duarte arrived?"

She shook her head. "Not yet, but the plaintiff's side just got here. I put them in the same conference room you were in yesterday. How do you think it's going?"

"Nothing's surprised me so far. What we heard yesterday has been consistent with her side of the story, but there's no evidence Diego ran that stop sign. Even the police report leans toward our side."

"So, it should be over soon?" Alicia asked as she headed toward the door.

"I think so. I hope so." Diego's testimony shouldn't take over one day, even with significant cross-examination and, if needed, Nolan would be Monday morning. "Let me know when he gets here."

This was a simple case, and Harrison still hadn't figured out why the other side still thought they had a chance. Perhaps they'd hoped that Diego would just give up and let the insurance company settle.

No. That wasn't happening, Harrison decided; not with his client. Diego might not be rich and powerful, like other people Harrison represented, but he was a good man, and Troy's best friend, and Harrison would be damned if the law would mistreat him.

Diego arrived, and Alicia brought him to Harrison first so they could go over the day's line of questions. "All you need to do is tell them what happened that night. Don't answer any more than their questions, though. That's how they want to trip you up. Just stick with short, factual answers, and if something comes up that you're not sure about, ask to confer with me."

The young man nodded but looked terrified in his best suit, his curly hair plastered to his head. "I will. Thank you again." He took a drink from his bottle of water, his hand trembling. "I should be done after today?"

"Your part, yes, until we go to trial, if we don't get this settled out of court. Then Nolan will be on Monday and that should be it unless they provide any more witnesses. But I hope that her legal team will drop this when they figure out that one, they don't have a case, and two, we're not backing down. I know her attorney very well. He's not dumb, but this isn't the slam dunk case he thought he signed up for." Harrison glanced at the clock on his desk; it was time. It took him a minute to stand, and he moved gingerly. "Are you sure you don't want a counter-suit against her? I think our chances would be good. Very good," Harrison said as they walked to the door of his office.

Diego shook his head. "I just want this over. No more court, no more lawyers. No offence, Mr. Crawford," he said with a wry smirk. "You've been great, and I don't know how I'll ever thank you. But I just want all of this to be over."

Of course, that made sense, and it said a lot about this young man that he wasn't willing to use this opportunity to make a quick buck. And, in a way, this helped Harrison's relationship with Nolan. The sooner this case concluded, the easier it would be to pursue a romantic relationship with him.

Just a few more days.

Several people sat around a large rectangular wooden table in the main conference room, the plaintiff's attorney and staff on one side, with Harrison and the rest of Diego's team on the other. Harrison had a few interns with them, for some experience, and to help make their side look more imposing.

As expected, the questions had been predictable. Had Diego been drinking? Had he taken any drugs? How long had they been out partying? What was the condition of the roads? What was his experience driving in rainy weather? Their attempt to bring up his previous criminal charges from his youth went nowhere, and it was more and more apparent that their case was falling apart before their eyes.

"Are there any more questions for my client?" Harrison asked as the afternoon drew to a close.

Jim Ashton, the lawyer for the plaintiff, shook his head. "Thank you for your testimony today, Mr. Duarte. We will be back on Monday to pick up." Everyone stood. As their side began packing up, Jim looked at Harrison and nodded over to the side of the room to talk privately. "He's really not putting in a counterclaim?" he asked in a low voice, incredulous.

Harrison snorted. "He's a good kid. Just wants this done."

Jim shrugged. "Can't say I'm surprised, even so, I'm grateful. I think he'd have an excellent shot." Then he smiled and dropped his voice even lower. "Is he the one you're—" and made a sexual gesture with his hand.

Harrison froze, and it was a moment before he spoke, his voice dangerously low. "I don't think I understand your question."

Jim grinned salaciously. "A little bird told me you were fooling around with someone in this case. Don't worry, I'm not bringing it up in discovery. There's too much evidence against my client. That sort of nonsense wouldn't help our case, and I'm not a monster. But I get it; sometimes you just gotta let off some steam, am I right?"

"Mr. Crawford?" Alicia stood at the door as the others all headed out into the front lobby. "Your son called. He wanted me to make sure you checked your messages. And I put Mr. Duarte in your office."

"Thank you, Alicia." Then Harrison glanced back at Jim. "I'll see you on Monday."

Jim grabbed his briefcase. "Have a good weekend, Harrison." He nodded politely at Alicia as he walked past her.

She watched Harrison's face as they headed to his office. "Are you okay? You look like someone spooked you."

Harrison exhaled slowly—had he been holding his breath since Jim's comment? "I'm going to talk to Diego and check my messages. Can you hold all my calls for about fifteen minutes?"

"Yes sir, boss." She still looked worried but didn't press it further.

The chat with Diego went quick, his mood lighter now that his part for today had ended. "You did a great job," Harrison told the young man. "One step closer to being done with this case."

"Thanks again, Mr. Crawford. I don't know how I'll ever be able to pay you back for this." Diego glanced down at his phone to check the time. "I've got to run but—"

Harrison shooed him toward the door. "Go. We're done for today. I'll let you know what our next step will be after Monday."

Once Diego left the office, Harrison unbuttoned his jacket and set it on the chair, then ambled over and dropped onto his comfortable sofa. Yes, there were two voice messages from Troy, but he couldn't get Jim's question out of his head.

Is he the one you're—

It was out.

Harrison groaned and covered his face.

At least, people knew *something*. If a lawyer from another firm had heard gossip that Harrison was messing around with a young man on his case, then his own colleagues had to know as well. No one had said anything outright to Harrison, but... they had to know.

The beep from his phone shook him out of his dark thoughts.

Nolan: *Diego wants to go to Delirium for a little while tonight, just celebrate that he got through today without fainting. He said you were great! [heart emoji]*

Nolan: *Can you come?*

So much for the quiet night at home, snuggled up together.

But Troy's voicemail caught his attention. *Hey Dad, can we get together tonight? I got a meeting with Trevor Montana, a record producer who'll be in town this weekend. He said he can meet me tomorrow before our gig at Geronimo's. Do you have some time tonight to help me go over my business plan presentation? I'm sorry for being so last minute, but I thought I could do it on my own, and I'm not sure anymore. I'll bring dinner. Thanks!*

Harrison's parental instincts kicked into gear, that small pride in being needed by his son, even if it was just for legal advice. But helping Troy meant he'd have to change plans to see Nolan.

Then there was his foot, which still ached from that incident at the gym. Delirium was a great place and being invited out tonight fed Harrison's ego and made him feel good. But tonight, he'd just be that old man sitting there watching them all dance. Maybe tomorrow.

Harrison's first text message was for Troy. *I'll be home at six. It won't take long to look over it.*

His second message was for Nolan. *I can't make it tonight. Maybe you can come to my house on Saturday again?*

They were so close to being done with this case, and Jim's words still rang in his ears. Just one more week of being cautious, that's all it would take.

Just a few more days.

Because once this case was over, the entire world would know how Harrison felt about Nolan Reynolds, and he couldn't wait.

Chapter 21

"Wait—" Nolan stood in Diego's doorway, one hand on his hip, and his favorite going out shirt—dark blue with small embroidered pink flowers—still half-unbuttoned. "Troy said he's going out with his father tonight?" That made no sense.

Diego shrugged. "That's what he told me. They were doing something together tonight." Diego's mood had lightened a thousand percent since the previous afternoon. He couldn't keep the smile off his face until he spotted Nolan's confusion. "Wait—did you have plans with his dad?"

"Yeah, sort of." Nolan thought back to that conversation with Troy. Maybe he'd misunderstood something. "I mean, there was nothing definite, just that we'd get together. But I was going to talk to Troy at the club, too." Harrison's message made a little more sense now. "I guess I'll just see Harrison tomorrow at his house."

Diego sat down on his bed and frowned. "Has Mr. Crawford done that before? Cancel on you?"

Diego still called him Mr. Crawford—Nolan understood completely, but it just made that age gap between them even more noticeable. "No, this is the first time. I mean, we haven't been going out a lot. We're waiting until after your lawsuit is over." But that didn't change the worried expression on Diego's face. "Why?"

He shrugged. "I don't know, Nolan. Troy just mentioned to me once—he said that his dad didn't like being in public with you yet, and it wasn't because of the case. He thinks his dad's just not sure he wants to be outed yet."

Hmm. It made perfect sense—the invitation to his private home, where no one would see them. Yes, maybe Harrison needed more time to figure out how he wanted to live his life, and Nolan needed to be understanding. But it still hurt, like a slap in the face. *He doesn't want to be seen with me.*

"Hey." Diego's head poked out into the hallway as Nolan turned and headed back to his room. "I just don't want you to get hurt. I don't think that means he doesn't like you. You guys can still have a good time at his house tomorrow. You'll probably have a better time if it's just the two of you."

"Yeah." Nolan agreed, but with little enthusiasm.

Diego sighed and headed back to his room.

A good time. Yeah, they could have a great time. But was that all that Harrison wanted—a good time in bed? Some fun, no-strings attached sex, some lessons in gay fucking while he decided if this was the lifestyle he wanted?

Maybe Nolan had read the situation wrong—it wouldn't be the first time. Had he missed some clues? It felt like they'd been on that same wavelength, so comfortable with each other that the next step—being in a relationship—felt like a natural progression.

But maybe Harrison hadn't wanted that at all. If the only time that Nolan would see him would be at his house, then maybe what Diego said was right.

Harrison didn't want to be seen with him as his boyfriend.

Angry feelings welled up inside him. Nolan had only himself to blame. Harrison had made no promises; they were just dating. Casual dating, that's all it was, even if Nolan had felt something more for him. That was just typical of him, getting attached too quick, jumping the gun again.

Harrison had a right to be cautious. This was his whole life, and he had an important professional career and friends and family to consider, not just the needs of a young and emotional fuckbuddy who wanted his full attention.

Nolan's heart hurt, and he wanted to talk to Harrison right now. But it wasn't the right time. Nolan had plans tonight, and apparently, so did Harrison. This could wait until tomorrow evening. Nolan would go to his house, if that was still what he wanted, and they could talk about their future together and what it would look like.

Diana, Diego's sister, joined them that night, along with Javier , the drummer in Steel Horse. "It's been ages since I've been here," she said, and her long hair head bobbed in time to the music as they passed through the dance floor on the way to the bar at the back of the club. "Oh good, there's a table free," she said, and slid onto a bench.

Diego laughed. "That's because we're here so early."

Diana gave him a light punch on the shoulder. "Look, I'm sorry if leaving the house at ten PM is just too late for me. I can't swing with you cool cats and your crazy party hours." Diego was often the serious one, but he lightened up when Diana was around, and her facial expressions when she got after her brother brought everyone to tears with laughter.

"No, this is good. I don't want to be out too late either," Nolan said, and headed to the bar. The first round of drinks was on him. "Okay, a toast to Diego and maybe almost being done with this stupid lawsuit."

The five of them raised their glasses. "To Diego!"

"Do you think you won't have to go to court?" Javier asked, after Diego caught him and Diana up on the case.

Diego shrugged. "That's what my lawyer said. He'll be surprised if we get that far."

Picturing Harrison standing in a courtroom, tall and strong and smart as a whip, making his case in front of a judge and jury, made Nolan shiver in a good way. "I can't wait for Monday, so this can all be over for me. What was it like, having them ask all those questions?" he asked and sipped his Cosmopolitan.

Diego's eyes went wide, and his fingers tugged at the damp napkin wrapped around his soft drink. "It terrified me. It was just like you see on TV. They had five people on one side of the table, and we had six, including me. Most of them didn't talk, they just sat there and took notes or typed in their computer. And the court reporter, she typed on that little machine of hers. Sometimes they asked her to repeat what I had just said." He sighed and leaned back against his chair. "But it was just like Mr. Crawford had coached me. They asked the same questions he'd said they would, and I just told the truth and nothing more."

"Could you tell if they were trying to catch you in a lie?" Diana asked.

"Twice. They wanted to know if I'd been drinking, so they kept bringing that up, what I had drank, like I'd slip up and say that I'd had a beer or whatever. A lot of the same questions, but when it was over—" Diego waved his hands in front of him. "It was done, and Mr. Crawford said that they had found no weaknesses in our case."

Nolan imagined Harrison sitting at that table, defending Diego, not letting the plaintiff's team attack him. Harrison knew his shit around a courtroom, and it made Nolan proud. The idea of belonging to this smart, powerful man.

At least, if Harrison wanted him.

Nolan finished his Cosmo and ordered another. The club was getting crowded, and a few more friends joined them. It was too early to celebrate Diego's win, but it had been a long time since Nolan had seen his roomie so relaxed and confident, and his confidence made Nolan less nervous about Monday, when they scheduled his own testimony.

It turned out their timing was perfect because an hour later, Delirium was packed. Even from their table in the back the thump of the bass pounded in their chests, and they all swayed in their seats to the music.

"Hand to God, it was the worst tattoo I've seen in real life. The cat wasn't so bad, but it had human legs, I guess on purpose, and they were spread open—" Diego's hands indicated how big the tattoo was, but then his eyes went wide at the sight of something—no, someone behind Nolan. "Jake's here."

Nolan's stomach dropped. Delirium had never been Jake's regular spot, but since they'd broken up, Nolan hadn't seen him here once. But that didn't mean the man wasn't allowed to be here. Besides, Nolan had moved on. He'd see Harrison tomorrow, and they'd spend the night together, and talk about the future so that all these silly worries he made up in his head would go away.

Nolan was so lost in his thoughts, like always, that he didn't notice everyone looking behind him until—"Hey, Nolan."

He twisted his head around. "Jake," he said with a fake casualness to hide his shocked expression. Jake looked amazing, in a form-fitting black t-shirt and jeans so tight you could see the outline of his well-hung schlong. "How you doing?"

Jake smiled with his perfect teeth, bright white, that accented his golden tan, even in the club's darkness. "I'm great. I'm working at a new restaurant now and the tips have been good. In fact, I got a bonus today, so I thought I'd come celebrate."

"We're celebrating too," Diana said. "My brother—he had a good day."

Jake gave Diego a nod of his head, then turned to the bartender. "Can you give them all another round? Put it on my tab." He handed the bartender a credit card. "I'll just take a beer."

What happened to Jake? The man Nolan knew (and dated) never spent a cent on anyone besides himself and hadn't ever gotten along with Diego. But Nolan accepted the fresh drink. "Thanks," he said, and stood to give Jake a hug. Maybe he wasn't such a bad guy after all.

As they hugged, Jake dipped his head low and whispered in Nolan's ear. "You can thank me by coming home with me. I've missed you, babe."

A few months ago, this declaration of lust would've pleased Nolan to no end, and they'd be out of here and on our way back to Nolan's place. But nothing about Jake's offer interested him in the slightest anymore. "Sorry, I'm seeing someone now. And even if I wasn't—"

Jake chuckled. "Yeah, it's too late to go back. You always were smarter than me." He took a deep pull of his beer. "Then how 'bout you just dance with me, for old time's sake?" His eyes traveled up and down Nolan's body. "You look fucking good tonight."

Nolan's face got hot. Alarms went off in his head, but Jake was one of the best-looking people in this bar right now, and his words helped heal Nolan's bruised ego. "One dance, okay," he said, and set his drink down on the table. "I'll be back," he said to his friends, and ignored their worried expressions.

One dance wouldn't hurt.

Jake took Nolan's hand, and they pushed through the crowd toward the dance floor in the main room. Carving out a space among all the sweaty, swaying bodies, they danced.

Nolan closed his eyes and let the music flow through him. The last time he'd danced was when Harrison came out with them, the two of them moving together, learning each other's steps and rhythm. That memory made Nolan smile, but when he turned and it was Jake there, not Harrison, his smile faltered.

But he didn't want Jake either, so Nolan closed his eyes as he danced. Jake's hands settled on Nolan's hips, but he didn't push him off. They moved together to the beat of the dance music, pounding loud in his ears and in his chest. Then Jake turned Nolan's body, and pressed against him, Nolan's back to his chest. Jake bent his head and whispered, "I heard you got a new guy. Where is he?"

"Couldn't make it tonight," Nolan answered.

Jake tugged at one of his belt loops. "And he left you alone out here. Doesn't sound very smart to me."

"He's brilliant." *And he's not here,* the voice in Nolan's head reminded him. *He's at home because he doesn't want to be seen with you in public.* "I'm about done, I think." Nolan turned around to face Jake, but he was looking at someone else near the front door. "Thanks for the drinks—"

Suddenly, Jake's hands cupped Nolan's face and pulled him in for a kiss.

Nolan froze in shock, then pressed his hands against Jake's chest and roughly pushed him away. "What the *hell,* Jake?" Nolan asked.

"What? I thought you wanted it," Jake said, his arms wrapping tighter around Nolan.

Nolan stepped back away from him, disgusted. "Just go away." Fuck, what was he thinking, even getting close to that jerk again? Nolan stepped off the dance floor as fast as he could and headed back to his friends, who'd migrated to the back patio bar.

Diana's eyebrows lifted into her hairline when she saw Nolan's expression. "You okay?" she asked and slid over to make room for him.

"Yeah, just—" Nolan shuddered. "I forgot how gross that asshole always made me feel about myself." When he compared that to how Harrison made him feel—cherished and precious—there was no contest. "Diego, I think I'm gonna head home a little early." Nothing about the club appealed to Nolan tonight. He glanced down at his phone to check the time. If it wasn't too late, maybe he could call Harrison and just talk to him about his day, and just hear that low, growly voice telling him how much they needed each other.

But when Nolan got home that night, Harrison didn't answer his call or text, so Nolan went to bed worried that something might be wrong.

Understatement of the century.

Chapter 22

"Well, what do you think?" Troy's hands fidgeted on the table after Harrison went over the business plan that he'd created for Saturday's meeting with their potential music producer. "What else do we need?" he asked and pulled another slice of pizza onto his plate.

After Harrison reread over his business plan, he pulled off his reading glasses and set them down and rubbed the bridge of his nose. "It's good, Troy." And it was. The plan that Troy and his friends had developed to turn their band into a business was well laid-out and reasonable. Troy himself understood what it would take to make it to the next level in recording music. He had a sound concept of the potential pitfalls and how they might avoid them.

Hell, he'd even arrived with a large pepperoni pizza and a six-pack of Shiner Bock. "My biggest concern is your plan to use social media as your primary marketing tool and not a dedicated PR firm, but that may be just me being out of touch with the way they market local music." Kids these days, they used their phones for everything, including work and business. "You know I'll always be around if you want help with the financials. I might not know Instagram, but I can figure out your balance sheet."

"I really appreciate this, Dad. You don't know how much. But Trevor Montana is a big name in music production on the West Coast, and when he called and said he'd be at our show tomorrow night and wanted to talk beforehand, I got excited. I want to show this to him and let him know that we're serious about taking the band to the next level. I'm not saying that we're going to make it big, but…"

"And I'm glad you asked me to help you. I know you're grown up and have your own life, but I enjoy being a part of it, however I can. You can always come ask me for help." Harrison glanced down at his watch. "Even at ten PM on a Friday night," he grinned.

But Troy didn't laugh back at his joke. "I'm sorry if I messed up any plans you had tonight. I didn't think it would take this long." He paused a beat and pulled his laptop toward him. "You still seeing Nolan?" His voice wavered as his laptop snapped closed.

Harrison couldn't hide the smile on his face. "Yeah. I think he's coming over tomorrow after work." They hadn't seen each other in several days, and just the thought of having Nolan in his arms soon made Harrison's heart—and other parts of his body—tingle with excitement. But he wasn't about to share that much with his son. "One of these days, all of you guys should come over, and we can grill outside. If it's not too uncomfortable for you," Harrison added, still not sure how they'd navigate these waters.

But Troy just smiled. "Sounds good, Dad."

Maybe things would be okay after all. Harrison rubbed Troy's head like he used to when he was a child and then started clearing their dinner plates and empty pizza box from the table. He tossed them in the trash and headed back toward Troy. "I'm not sure what your schedule looks like, but I thought that maybe this summer we—"

Harrison stopped in his tracks. Troy stood frozen in place next to the table. His eyes, wide in his pale face, were locked on his phone screen. "What's wrong?" But Troy didn't speak, and Harrison's paternal instincts kicked in. "Troy, is everything okay?"

When he finally moved, his shoulders slumped at his sides. "Um, Dad…" Eyes downcast, he bit his lip and set his phone down on the table, screen-side down. "I don't know what to do." Then his eyes, so much like Harrison's own eyes, glanced up, filled with anguish. "I don't want to hurt you."

"Troy. Tell me what's going on?" Nothing felt worse than seeing his son in pain, and whatever was on that phone had done it. Harrison reached for it. "Let me—"

"Dad, wait." Troy grabbed it first and held it to his chest. "Uh, shit. Okay." The screen had gone black, so he unlocked it and handed it to Harrison. "Someone just sent me that link."

Harrison's heart pounded as he looked down at the screen. "Is that your Instagram?" He recognized Delirium, with its packed dance floor filled with bodies pressed against each other. But then— "Oh."

All the air left his lungs as he stared at the post.

It was Nolan.

Nolan, his eyes closed and shirt half-open, leaning back against another man. The other guy looked like a model from those old romance novels—tall, with shoulder-length blond hair and muscles everywhere. He hung his head back as if in the throes of sexual pleasure, his hands tight on Nolan's hips, Nolan pulled flush against his groin.

"Maybe it's his brother," Troy said, but even as he spoke the words, they both knew that wasn't true.

This was the man Harrison had fallen in love with, dancing—no, grinding with someone else. "Is this it?"

Troy shook his head. "Scroll left."

Harrison wished he hadn't. The next photograph showed the other man's hands grasping Nolan's torso. The last one —his stomach lurched at the last one—Nolan's body turned toward the other man, and their lips pressed against each other.

"Okay. Well, um..." What was he supposed to say? "Thank you for showing me this. Um, I think—"

Troy took the phone back and shoved it into his pocket. "Dad, I'm sorry. I shouldn't have—"

"No, don't be sorry. I needed to see that, right? I mean—" A bitter laugh escaped from his lips. "I think I need to be alone right now. I'm sorry, Troy." Harrison stood and put his arm around him. "Let's talk more tomorrow about your plan, okay? Don't forget your laptop."

Troy shook his head. "Are you sure? I can stay if you need."

"No, I'm going to go shower and go to bed. I'm okay, it's alright." There it was, that stupid laugh again even as his heart broke in two. "We were just friends, just messing around. It's no big deal," Harrison lied. "Don't be upset. I'll call you tomorrow."

It took another five minutes to convince Troy to leave, but soon it was just Harrison.

Alone in his house with his thoughts. Again.

He stood in the shower; his eyes screwed tight as the steaming water poured over his head. But his body stayed tense, that sick feeling in his stomach not going away. Was this who Nolan was when Harrison wasn't around? Maybe he had been wrong about their relationship and had given it more importance than Nolan had. Harrison couldn't be angry, could he, if they'd never discussed seeing other people.

Nolan was young and sexual and had a right to be with whomever he wanted. But that wasn't who Harrison was, and if Nolan needed that every night, then Harrison wasn't the one for him, and Nolan wasn't the one for him.

It felt like grief, the mourning of a relationship that had just begun, but had so much potential. They hadn't done more than spend one incredible night together, but Harrison had already thought that Nolan could be an important part of his life, someone who Harrison could build a future with.

Stupid. Even thinking about that now was ridiculous, just the dreams of a silly old man who had his head turned by a sexy young man who, by his own admission, flirted with everyone. Nolan was just being friendly to a fool who had fallen in love with the first man who showed him any attention.

Stupid, stupid Harrison.

Chapter 23

Nolan: *Hey, is everything okay? I left a message on your voicemail. Call me when you get this. I just wanted to make sure we're still on for tonight. I packed a bag and brought some going out clothes if you want to go see the band play at Geronimo's. See you soon [heart emoji]*

Harrison hadn't called back by the time Nolan headed into work and hadn't responded to any of his text messages. Worry lingered in the back of his head, that maybe Harrison had been in an accident or had hurt himself, but if that were the case, Troy would let Nolan know, right? Troy wouldn't keep that from him.

But Nolan hadn't talked to Troy either. He never made it out to the club last night, or if he had, it was after Nolan went home. He hated spending any more time with Harrison without hashing it out with Troy first, getting it all out on the table, but Nolan wasn't going to stop seeing Harrison. His heart skipped at the thought of being in his arms tonight, all night long.

Nolan was in too far to get out now, no matter what Troy thought about it.

His lunch break rolled around at two, and still no word from Harrison. Maybe he lost his phone, Nolan decided.

Maybe it fell into the pool. Nolan spent the morning checking every few minutes for a message. Finally, just as he sat down in the small lounge area to heat up his leftover chicken pad thai, his phone vibrated in his pants pocket.

Finally. Nolan let out a long breath and pulled the phone out, only to frown when Diego's name appeared on the text message. *Call me as soon as you get this.*

Nolan's throat went dry. Had something happened? This all had to be related. The only other person in the break room was Tammy, a sweet older Asian woman who did manicures. She had her headphones in and was watching something on her phone. Nolan's fingers shook as he pressed Diego's name and the green phone icon.

He answered right away. "What happened?" Nolan asked, not giving him a chance to say anything. Silence on the other end worried him for a moment. "Are you there?"

"Yeah, I'm here. Look, Nolan, I don't know who did this but—" Diego paused, and sighed. "Someone took some pictures of you and Jake at the club, dancing together. I don't know but looks like you're kissing him." There was a long pause. "Troy showed them to his dad."

Everything stopped, except this buzzing noise in his head. "I didn't kiss him."

"I don't know what to tell you, man. The pictures don't look good."

"You saw them?" Nolan's voice was just above a whisper.

"Yeah. Look, I'm gonna send you the link." Another pause. "I'm sorry this happened to you. It stinks."

"Yeah. Um, thanks, Diego. I'm going to fix this, don't worry. Oh hey—" Nolan was about to hang up when he remembered. "Good luck tonight. I'm not sure if I'm going to make it."

"You take care of whatever you need." Diego ended the call, and Nolan sat frozen in his chair for another minute, until his phone vibrated again. It was the link.

It was a hundred times worse than Nolan thought.

Jake's hands were on his body, holding him. It must have been taken the second that Jake tried to kiss him. Of course, it didn't show when Nolan pushed him away, or stormed off the dance floor. But it showed enough, and now he understood why Harrison hadn't called back.

The second half of Nolan's shift dragged on, and all he wanted was to leave, to get away from the bright lights and loud music. Even Angel's cheery voice answering the phones irritated him, and he overheard her apologize to a customer for his grumpy attitude that day.

Before Nolan left, he stopped by her counter, and tapped it with his fingers. "I'll see you on Tuesday."

Her wary smile hurt his heart, but Nolan deserved it. "I hope you feel better, Nolan. Oh, and good luck on Monday," she added.

Monday.

The deposition was on Monday.

Fuck.

Nolan slumped into his apartment, with his overnight bag tossed over his shoulder like a bag of rocks. No, a bag of failure, the physical embodiment of another relationship in the toilet, tanked before it even began. After Nolan took the dogs out, he sat in his room and watched them play on the floor while he examined the photographs more closely.

They'd been posted on Delirium's Instagram account, which struck Nolan as odd but not necessarily nefarious. Those three pictures had been among several posted; it wasn't like they singled Nolan out. But he and Jake had been the focus of those three particular photographs, and judging from the timestamps, someone had told Troy about them as soon as they were uploaded.

The whole situation stank, like Diego said, but Nolan couldn't deny that was him in the pictures. It hurt, like someone punched him in the gut, but it was true. Nolan had danced with Jake, and let Jake touch him, and because of that, Nolan lost the best man he'd ever known.

The idea crossed Nolan's mind to drive to Harrison's house and make him listen to whatever excuse he could make, but he didn't. If Nolan wanted to be a grown up, then he had to act like a grown up. One last message, and the ball was in Harrison's court.

Nolan: *I don't have any excuse for what you saw, but it wasn't what you think. Please call me so we can talk. You mean the world to me, Harry. Don't give up on me.*

Harrison never called. The puppies slept with Nolan that night, and their tongues licked the tears off his face as he fell asleep.

Chapter 24

Harrison spent Saturday in a daze, slinking from room to room, but not much got done. After reading the same page three times, he closed the book he'd tried to read, and none of the college basketball games on his big screen television held his interest.

But Harrison's chore list hadn't changed just because his heart was broken. After tossing and turning all night, he woke up Sunday morning, slugged down two cups of strong coffee, and got to work with all the tasks that needed to be done. He'd planned on cleaning out the garage, currently filled to the rafters with boxes and boxes of Jenny's old clothes, and decorations for the house that he didn't want to keep. Troy would be by later this afternoon to help and then take the boxes to his mother's new apartment.

The work was monotonous, but it helped take his mind off his worries, and before Harrison knew it, it was close to lunchtime. It had been an easier task than he'd thought, since most of it was just pulling out boxes that wouldn't be re-entering the garage. Physical labor, that helped too. Harrison's shirt, drenched with sweat, clung to his body, and with each box of shit that reminded him of the past hefted out of his garage, the better he felt about moving on.

The boxes of Jenny's things hadn't made him miss her. That part of his life was done, and Harrison was at peace with it. They'd had a good run and raised a good man. But Harrison didn't want to grow old with her.

For a moment, he had even thought Nolan might be— *No*. Harrison put those thoughts away.

Back to work, where he lost himself in the task at hand— cleaning, and re-organizing plastic bins, emptying the clutter and filling boxes to donate to charity.

When Troy's car pulled into the driveway, Harrison was almost done. He smiled and waved at his son just as Troy spotted the open garage door and walked toward him. "Hey, Dad."

"Hi." Harrison plastered a bright smile on his face. "What's up?"

Troy shrugged. "I just wanted to check in on you, see how you were doing." Troy nodded, his eyes tracking all over the garage. "I thought I'd help you out, but it looks like you got a head start on me."

"I'm fine. Really." Harrison leaned in for a one-armed hug, though he kept his distance because he didn't want to get Troy dirty. "Just about ready for a break, though. Can you stay for lunch?" Troy nodded again, but the smile on his face didn't quite reach his eyes. "Great. Let me take a quick shower. You want to order something, or we can just make sandwiches?"

"Sandwiches are great. You go shower and I'll get everything ready."

Something was wrong with his son. "Are you okay?" Harrison asked, almost glad that he had something else to take his mind off Nolan and that ache in his heart. But Harrison didn't want to see his son hurting, either. "Is this about what happened?"

Troy shook his head. "Go shower. We can talk afterward."

Twenty minutes later, Harrison made it to the kitchen. Troy had laid out all the sandwich makings and had sat down at the table, and his blank eyes stared at his phone. "What's going on?" Harrison asked and sat down next to him. As much as his heart ached, Troy was his son, and his needs would always come first. "I know you came over here to help me, but I'm more worried about you."

Troy blinked, and Harrison's worry doubled. "Troy?"

"I'm sorry, Dad." His lip quivered. "It's my fault."

Harrison froze. "What do you mean? What happened?"

He took a few deep breaths before he spoke. "It was Mom. She asked me to—fuck, sorry, I just..." His voice trailed off, and he avoided Harrison's eyes.

But Troy's words had Harrison's hackles up. *Jenny.* His voice dropped an octave. "What did your mom do, Troy?"

Troy wrung his hands as he spoke. "She said that Nolan would hurt you and that your job was at stake. She said that you were too close to see it, and that you were going to get hurt in the long run."

"What did she do?" Harrison repeated. "Troy. Tell me."

He took a breath and lifted his face, looking Harrison straight in the eye. "She asked me to keep you busy on Friday night and make sure you didn't go to the club or see Nolan. I didn't know exactly what she'd had planned, but it was something about making you see Nolan's true character."

Harrison's face fell.

Troy continued. "I didn't think—I mean, I know she didn't like him and didn't want you two together, but I couldn't imagine Nolan would do that to you."

Harrison put the picture together in his mind. "How did she know he'd be dancing with that guy?"

Troy swallowed hard. "I'm still not sure about this part, but I'm guessing she found out who he used to date and paid the guy to go to the club that night and hit on Nolan. Make it look like they were back together, or at least make it look like Nolan was cheating."

"Jesus. I don't understand. What does she care who I date? I mean, forget what she said about my job and career. Let's be real, Troy. She doesn't give a shit about my job.

She'd love to see me knocked on my ass. What's really behind this?"

Troy hung his head before speaking. "I went to see her this morning before I came here, to tell her what a shitty thing this was, and that it pissed me off, how she got me involved." Troy took another deep breath, his voice shaky with emotion. "Things aren't working out with her and Bill. I don't know if they broke up or if she just sees the writing on the wall, but—" Troy covered his face. "She was up to something, and I should have told her no. I'm so sorry. I never wanted to hurt you, Dad."

Jennifer. Harrison leaned back in his chair and folded his hands. As insane as the plan sounded, it made perfect sense if she wanted to keep hurting Harrison, and what a way to do it.

But right now, his priority was his son. "First, Troy, thank you for telling me what happened. I'm sad to say that her plan worked. I don't know what Nolan's side of the story is, and I'm sure I'll find out later. But I accept your apology."

Troy sniffed and leaned against him, and they hugged tight. "I'm so sorry," he repeated.

"I know. I don't know what to say about your mother right now, so let's just leave it alone for a bit." Harrison was still in shock that Jenny dragged Troy into this, and that Troy had helped her.

But Troy had been taken advantage of by his mother and berating him now wasn't going to help his son. Instead, Harrison kissed the side of Troy's head. "Okay, it's out, and we both know. We're good." Harrison rubbed Troy's shoulder, and they sat in silence for a moment. "Let's have a sandwich, and then you can help me finish up the garage." Harrison stopped with a start. "Hey, how was your gig last night? Did the presentation go okay?"

Troy managed a weak smile. "I think he liked what we had to say, and the gig went well. Standing room only at the club, and people had a good time."

"Well, that's great news." Harrison hugged him again, and as they ate, Troy talked more about his meeting with the music producer.

Later that afternoon, after Troy left with the boxes for his mother, Harrison walked into the kitchen and pulled a bottle of beer from the fridge. He'd left a pair of swimming trunks on the porch, so after a quick change he sat in the jacuzzi and let the hot water wash away his sadness.

Harrison looked at all of Nolan's messages, filled with excitement about being together this weekend, and those silly heart emojis he used. Then that last message, asking Harrison to call him.

But Harrison hadn't called. Instead, he'd convinced himself that they were wrong for each other, that they hadn't felt anything real for each other, and their time together had been fun, but that was all.

A bit of fun.

That was for the best, really. Nolan was twenty-seven, too young for Harrison, and for fuck's sake, Harrison hadn't even been officially divorced for more than a few weeks. What was he thinking—that he'd fall in love with the first person who wanted him? That love was that easy?

It had felt good, being wanted by someone so young and beautiful, but it wasn't love. Couldn't be.

The man that Nolan had danced with was who he should be with, someone like that, youthful and handsome. Why on earth would Harrison saddle him down to someone older like him? What did Harrison have to offer? He couldn't be angry with Nolan's choice.

Twice Harrison picked up his phone to call Nolan and hear his side of the story, even though he knew it already. Nolan had been tricked, yes, but he'd danced with the other man, no doubt about that. But Harrison also knew that if he talked to Nolan, he'd want Nolan here with him, and that wasn't what either of them needed.

How could Harrison trust Nolan with his heart if this was what happened when he couldn't be around? Sure, they hadn't made any promises to each other, but even so, a stinging sharpness at the corner of Harrison's eyes made him feel dumb.

He set his phone back down.

Was not responding immature? Yes, but Harrison didn't care. Even as the day passed into evening, Harrison realized that this had been the only possible outcome, and better that it happened sooner rather than later. He was always going to be too old for Nolan.

Their differences, which had been exciting at first, would never let them be happy together. The sooner Harrison accepted that, the sooner he could get back to his normal life.

Chapter 25

Sunday mornings were Nolan's day off, and he often slept in. But it was still dark when his eyes blinked open, and before he could tell himself 'No,' he reached for the phone.

No message from Harrison.

Nolan dropped the phone on the floor next to his bed, covered his face with a pillow, and tried to go back to sleep.

It must have worked. When his eyes opened again, sunlight poured in through his bedroom window. Sounds from the television in the living room meant Diego was up, so Nolan dragged himself out of bed and padded down the hall. Diego had been disappointed that Nolan hadn't gone to see his band play the previous night, but Nolan couldn't go anywhere where he'd run into Troy, not until he'd cleared things up with Troy's dad.

Nolan couldn't imagine what Troy thought of him. His face burned with embarrassment every time he remembered those pictures.

Diego sat cross-legged on the sofa and ate a bowl of cereal with the puppies at his feet. "Morning." Diego glanced down at the dogs. "I took them out already."

Nolan tried to smile, and settled on the floor next to the dogs, who scampered onto his lap. "Thanks, man. How did it go last night?"

"Good, I think. We met up with Trevor Montana, and he seemed to like the show." Diego scooped cereal into his mouth as he talked about how well the band played. "Not sure if he wants to sign us up yet, but I think he liked what he saw."

"That's great." Bandit rolled over onto his back, and Nolan scratched his belly. Diego looked over expectantly, but Nolan shook his head. No sense in pretending that he wasn't devastated. "I haven't talked to him."

Diego sighed. "Fuck. I was hoping you guys would've at least texted by now."

"Me too. But I won't hound him. If he doesn't want to talk to me anymore, he doesn't have to." Nolan had picked up his phone to call Harrison several times since that last text, then changed his mind. It was Harrison's choice.

"But tomorrow's your deposition," Diego said, that worry back in his voice.

Fuck. Only having his heart ripped apart could make Nolan forget about the looming deposition. "I fucked this all up, didn't I?"

"Look, Nolan..." Diego got up and set his empty bowl in the sink before returning to the living room. "You were right about Mr. Crawford. He won't tank my case just because you hurt him. But he deserved better than what he got. And I know this isn't what you wanted, and that it's not fair to you either. But let's just get through today and tomorrow and then see what happens, okay?"

Nolan appreciated Diego's level-headedness with this situation. *He has every right to be pissed at me right now.* "Yeah. After tomorrow, it might not be an issue anymore if he doesn't want to be with me."

"And what are you going to do if that is what he decides?" Diego asked.

Nolan furrowed his brow. "What do you mean?"

Diego sat on the arm of the sofa, looking down at him, and frowned. "The last time your heart took a beating, it was a month before you snapped out of your bad mood, and even then, it was only because I dragged your ass out of here. I just don't want this to start again, you not getting up and going out and living your life because you're sad."

Harsh words, but accurate. "Yeah. But—" Nolan looked up at him. "It wasn't just Jake that had me upset. I think more of it was not getting that job. I really wanted it."

Diego's eyes widened slightly. "I didn't know that."

"Yeah. I didn't say much about it because it embarrassed me, getting passed over. But you're right. I can't let getting dumped every few months dictate my life. I need to do something for myself." He took a deep breath and let it out slowly. "I haven't said anything to anyone"—Except Harrison, his heart reminded him—"but I'm enrolling at San Jacinto next semester to finish my degree."

Diego's hand rested on Nolan's shoulder and gave him a squeeze. "That's great, man. Anything I can do to help, you just let me know, yeah?"

Nolan held his hands out, and Diego pulled him up off the floor. "I think I'll start with a shower."

Diego laughed. "I'd hoped you say that."

Noah: *You okay? I heard some shit went down.*
Noah: *I'm at the coast with Martin this weekend but let me know if you need anything.*
Nolan: *Thanks, I'm okay.*
Noah: *[thumbs up emoji]*

Nolan headed to his mother's house for lunch. It was just the two of them, and a quiet lunch without Noah around picking fights. "I can't believe how big those dogs have gotten," Dani said after Nolan shared photos from his phone. "They look strong and healthy."

Nolan nodded toward her back room, where her latest group of puppies squawked loudly. "These border collies are so big already." Had it just been two weeks since he'd been over here last, talking with Noah and Chance about deworming dogs and his newest crush? Two weeks when he'd had his first date with Harrison, shared their first kiss and gone back to Nolan's place for another first for him.

Two weeks, and Nolan managed to screw it up.

If Dani noticed his bleaker-than-normal mood, she said nothing. "They're getting a lot of attention already on the websites. I think they'll be adopted quick once they've gotten the okay from Doctor Chance." She spooned broccoli onto his plate. "We had a couple interested in Smokey, but the background check didn't go through."

"That's a shame," Nolan said, and reached for a piece of baked chicken. Their organization was thorough with who adopted their dogs. "But I hope they go together."

"Me too, but two pit bulls are a lot of dog to handle. You'd need someone with a lot of space and time to work with them." They made some small talk about Nolan's job, but toward the end of the meal, she came out and asked, "Honey, are you doing okay?"

Nolan nodded. "Yeah. Just—" It had always been hard keeping things from his mom. Noah could make up stories she'd believe, but she always, always read Nolan like a book. "Me and the guy I was seeing... I don't think it's going to work out after all."

Her eyes darkened with genuine sadness. "Oh baby, I'm sorry." She took another bite of her chicken. "This is—this was the older gentleman?"

Nolan snickered. *Of course, she found out.* "You make it sound like he was elderly or something. But yes, it was him. He thinks—" Nolan bit his lip. This wasn't anything he'd wanted to talk about with his mother, at least not now. "We had a good time, but it wasn't meant to be."

She nodded. "Sometimes that happens. But you're an amazing man, and I'm sure if you want to find someone, he'll be out there."

Nolan snorted. "I hope so. But maybe I just need to not worry about that for a while."

She tilted her head and caught his eye. "What does that mean?"

"I think I'm going to take a page from Noah's book and spend a little time bettering myself. I'm applying to get back into college," he said, and took another bite of chicken. "This is fantastic. Did you use paprika?"

Bless her. Dani tried to contain her joy, but she couldn't, and pulled Nolan into a tight hug while he was still eating. "Nolan, I'm so happy to hear that. Let me know if there's anything you need or help with tuition. I want to help."

It was worth anything to see her smile like that. "I will, I promise. And thanks."

She touched his cheek. "Does Noah know?"

Nolan laughed. "Not yet. I wanted to make sure that they accepted me before I told him. Otherwise, I'd never hear the end of it."

Dani shook her head. "He'll be another supporter, just you watch. He wants what's best for you. We all do."

Nolan had the best family, he really did. "I know. And you're right. I'll tell him when he gets back. Maybe next weekend I'll ask him to look over my application essay."

With support like this, Nolan had no excuse not to succeed. They were all right. Finding someone to love was important, but he couldn't let his broken heart stop him from moving forward and growing up.

Chapter 26

Twice on Sunday night Harrison picked up his phone, his finger hovering over Jim Ashton's number. They had to reschedule Nolan's deposition—how was he going to spend the day sitting next to Nolan, questioning him, assisting him while answering Jim's questions? Harrison could plead illness, or maybe just call in to work altogether and spend another day at home.

But doing what? Moping around, feeling sorry for himself?

No. This had to get done Monday—for Diego's sake, for Nolan's sake, and for Harrison himself. The sooner this case ended, the faster they could all get on with their lives. That is what they all needed.

And with any luck, they'd finish this mess tomorrow afternoon.

Sometime around three in the morning Harrison woke up with an idea, how he'd solve his problem. Harrison couldn't sleep after that, just tossed and turned until his alarm went off. No workout that morning. Harrison skipped the gym and headed into the office early to set his plan in motion.

When Alicia walked in and spotted Harrison at his desk, she greeted him with her customary broad smile. "Hello, early bird. Did you have a good weekend?"

Harrison halted at her comment, then remembered—when he'd left on Friday, he'd been lighter than air at his weekend plans. She couldn't know what sad events had transpired during that time. "A lot happened. I got some bad news, but I think it will all be okay in the end." Before she could respond, Harrison added, "Can you ask Ben Barton if he can see me? It's sort of an emergency. And I'll need to speak with Diego Duarte, if possible, in the next twenty minutes."

Her eyes widened. "Yes, sir." She nodded once before she left, and Harrison slumped in his chair, exhausted already just thinking about the day ahead of him, and the conversations to be had.

Did Harrison have the strength to do this?

A minute later, the intercom buzzed. "Mr. Barton has time for you right now. He's in his office."

Harrison grabbed his phone, slid it into his coat pocket, and headed down the hall toward Ben's office. Rocco, his assistant, nodded at the door and indicated that Harrison should just go inside. Okay. Two deep breaths, and he knocked twice and opened the door.

Ben stood at his large glass window, similar to the one in Harrison's office with a steaming coffee mug in his hand as he looked out over downtown. "Mornin' Crawford. What seems to be the trouble?" he asked with a grin.

Harrison's feet were heavy as he walked toward him. "Hey Ben. Um, I've got a favor to ask, and it's a big one."

The wide smile dropped from his face. "Whatever you need, Harrison. Just tell me."

So, he did.

When Nolan arrived, Alicia took him straight into the conference room. Yes, it was a chicken shit move, but Harrison couldn't bring him into his office before the deposition started. With any other client, Harrison would have gone over their testimony one last time and done his best to dissipate any last-minute nerves. But Harrison's own feelings were too raw and on the surface to be alone with Nolan right now, much less talk to him before this was all settled and done.

Instead, Harrison pawned him off on Jania. She could answer any last-minute questions Nolan had and made sure that he was prepared for the day.

But at nine AM, Harrison couldn't wait any longer. One more deep breath, and he headed into the conference room. "My apologies for being late," Harrison said, and looked around. Everyone was already seated and ready to go. Nolan's pale face stood out in his dark blue suit, those expressive gray eyes more sad than scared. Harrison's heart ached, and he avoided looking in Nolan's direction. "I'd like to thank everyone for being here early on a Monday morning." Harrison stood behind his chair, and he gripped the wooden frame. "If you don't mind, I'd like to say something before today's deposition begins."

Everyone turned to look at each other when Harrison didn't sit down. "Is everything okay?" Jim asked.

"It will be." There was a knock at the conference door, and Ben stepped inside. "For anyone here who doesn't know Ben Barton, he's the senior partner at this law office and a good friend. I asked him this morning if he'd step in and take over my role in these proceedings today, and if needed, tomorrow." Every eye in the room was on Harrison. Nolan's terrified expression was hard to miss, but Harrison stayed focused on the others.

Jim cleared his throat. "I think I speak for everyone when I say that I hope things are okay with you, Harrison. Is this change of representation okay with your client?"

Harrison nodded. "I have briefed Mr. Duarte on the change, and he understands. Both he and I are confident that Mr. Barton will represent him with integrity and fidelity. As for me, I've—" Harrison stopped and took a deep breath. "I'm recusing myself due to some personal feelings that have developed between myself and a witness for my client. My recusal in no way, shape, or form should suggest any impropriety to the substance of the legal case. But I believe that someone who doesn't have an intimate or emotional connection to anyone involved in this case, as I currently do, would better represent my client."

The court reporter fingers moved silently against her machine, and when Harrison paused, she paused as well, and looked up at him, a small smile on her face.

"Thank you," Harrison said to her, and to the rest of the room. "Mr. Barton has been briefed on the status of Mr. Reynolds' deposition. I'll be in my office if something should come up."

Jim Ashton glanced over at Nolan, and back at Harrison as he stepped away from the table to make room for Ben, who took his place at the center chair.

Ben's deep voice rang out as the door closed behind Harrison. "Alright folks, let's get this here started today."

Chapter 27

*H**oly shit.*
That was not how Nolan expected his morning to go.

The deposition itself went off without a hitch. Just like Harrison said, both sides asked very similar questions, and Nolan answered truthfully and honestly and didn't deviate from what he'd previously stated in his pre-trial interviews. But his heart raced in his chest the entire time as he waited for the other side's lawyer to bring up his relationship with Harrison. Anyone who looked in Nolan's direction when Harrison was in the room could see that he was the one; Nolan's entire body radiated panic. Would they ask him if they were dating, or even worse—if there had been any physical intimacy?

Nolan couldn't lie, but also—he didn't know how to answer. *Yes, but not anymore. Yes, but we broke up.*

Yes, but he didn't want me.

Nolan's testimony wrapped up by lunch, and both sides agreed that he wasn't needed any more that day. "You mean, that's it?" he asked as everyone stood and gathered their belongings and laptops.

"Yes sir, Mr. Reynolds." Mr. Barton, the lawyer who took over for Harrison, reached over and shook his hand. "You did an outstanding job today. You are roommates with Diego, correct?" After Nolan nodded, he added, "If you talk to him this afternoon, let him know that someone from our office should be in touch with him today, hopefully with good news."

Okay. Nolan wasn't sure what that meant but wasn't about to stick around and find out. Even without his morning cup of coffee, adrenaline pumped through his body, and his pulse probably wouldn't start to go down until his feet were planted firmly on the pavement outside this office building for the last time.

Wait. Was this his last time here? That cold realization hit like a punch in the gut. Nolan didn't ever have a reason to come back, did he?

Not if Harrison wasn't in his life.

"Mr. Reynolds?"

Nolan looked up. A woman at the door smiled at him. Everyone had left, and he was the only one left in the conference room. "Um, Alicia, right?"

She nodded. "Yes, that's me. Can I help you?"

"I hope so." As Nolan approached her, he took a deep breath. "Will he see me? I'd really like to talk to him if he's got a moment."

Her eyes softened. She was his ally, Nolan understood, and right now he needed all the help he could get. "Let me check. Wait right here." She walked off in the direction of Harrison's office, and after a moment, she stepped out and waved him over. "He can see you now."

Finally.

Nolan whispered, "Thank you," to her as he passed, and swore he saw hope in her eyes. He knocked twice and opened the door—but Harrison wasn't at his desk. "Hello?" Nolan called out as his eyes searched the room.

"Over here." Harrison sat on the sofa, close to the large glass windows where they'd first talked. Was that just a few weeks ago? Everything in Nolan's life had changed since that day, and now, his heart thumped fast in his chest as he walked over there again and prayed that this wasn't the end.

Nolan tried to sound calm and collected, even if he felt anything but that. Settling on the far side of the sofa, they faced each other for the first time since it happened. "You surprised me today. Wasn't expecting that."

One corner of Harrison's mouth tugged up in a half-hearted smile. He'd undone his tie and the first couple of buttons of his shirt. "Honestly, I wasn't either. Just sort of occurred to me this morning."

"How come?" Nolan leaned back, crossing one leg over the other. "Were you worried about getting into trouble or something?"

Harrison shook his head. "Not like that. Diego's not going to lose the case, no matter what happened between us. But I couldn't stand up there and talk to you and look at you—" He stopped and pressed his lips together tightly. "At least, not today. And that wasn't fair to Diego. He deserved someone focused on getting the job done, so I asked my partner to take my place."

That made sense. A minute passed, and neither of them spoke. Finally, Nolan reached out and rested his hand on top of Harrison's fingers. He didn't pull away. "I'm sorry about what happened. I didn't mean for any of that to hurt you."

"I know." After a moment, Harrison pulled his hand back to his lap. "It was a trap, and we both fell into it."

What? "What do you mean, a trap?"

All the air seemed to leave Harrison's body. "You didn't hear? My ex-wife was behind it all. She set you up—arranged for your ex-boyfriend to be with you, and to take those pictures."

Nolan's eyes shut tight. "And I walked straight into it." *How stupid could I have been?* Of course, that's why Jake had shown up at that bar, why he'd been so nice to everyone, spending money. "I got a bonus at work," that's what he'd said.

And like a dummy, Nolan believed him.

"Nolan?"

He looked up. Harrison was watching him carefully. "Yeah. I'm okay. Just mad at myself."

"It's my fault she even brought you into this mess. It was me she wanted to hurt. You—" His sad smile was back. "Wounding you was just a bonus for her."

"Her lucky day." The idea that someone could be so cruel to a person she didn't really know, just to get back at another person, was hard for Nolan to believe. "I've got to admit, I'm impressed at the length she went through to do this. Finding Jake and then setting up the photographer. She'd even have to make some sort of arrangement with whoever ran Delirium's social media accounts. This wasn't cheap." Their eyes met again. "And it doesn't seem fair, letting her win."

Harrison nodded slowly. "Ah, but what if she was right? Maybe we're too different. No, listen, Nolan," he said, when Nolan tried to interrupt. "You've got your whole life ahead of you, and sooner or later, you're going to get tired of me. We both know that."

What? "Is that what's worrying you? That's why you're not calling me back?" These words shook Nolan. It wasn't about Nolan and Jake, or that Harrison thought Nolan wanted to be with someone else. No, Harrison saw the pictures and concluded they were wrong for each other in general. "I'm not crazy about the fact that you think you get to make that decision on your own, and not include me in it."

Harrison sat straight up, and his eyes widened as he took in Nolan's words. He held out a hand. "Wait—"

Nolan shook his head. "No, you wait. Is this because you think I'm some kid who doesn't know what he wants? You don't respect me enough to let me be part of this decision that might affect the rest of my life? Because I love you, you massive tool , and I'm not ready to let you go." Nolan didn't know what had gotten into him, but he'd had it.

His job, his brother, and his boyfriend—the most important decisions of Nolan's life had been made by other people, out of his hands. Now it was time he took control. "I deserve the chance to decide what I want, and I choose you." Nolan stood, angrier than he'd ever been in a long time. "I know what I want. I know who I am. When you figure out who you really are, Harrison Crawford, give me a call."

Nolan stormed out of the office and was in the elevator before he let out the breath he'd been holding. He pressed the button for the ground floor and smiled. Yes, it was Harrison's decision now, but Nolan had said his truth and could live with the consequences.

His part of this lawsuit was done, and it was time to get started with the rest of his life.

Chapter 28

He loves me, Harrison thought.
Nolan loves me.

Of course, it wasn't true. They hadn't even known each other a month. There was no way that Nolan could be in love with him, especially after he charged out of Harrison's office, his gray eyes flashing with rage.

But didn't Harrison do exactly what Nolan accused him of? Had Harrison decided that since Nolan was younger, that Harrison knew more than he did? Was Harrison just as bad as his friends and family, making that assumption that Nolan couldn't make that decision for himself?

But choosing Harrison wasn't the smart decision. Nolan was just starting out, and Harrison had one foot firmly planted in middle age. Hell, he could retire in ten years. What happened between them was pure attraction and curiosity. It couldn't be love.

Could it?

Maybe Nolan knew more about love than he did.

A knock at the door pulled Harrison out of his thoughts. "Mr. Crawford?" It was Alicia. "Can I get you anything?"

"Yes." Harrison walked back to his desk. Leaning against it, he took one long breath and let it out slow. "Would you get me the phone number for Noah Reynolds? He works at U of H, um, the big campus near downtown."

She smiled. "Will do." The door closed behind her as she left.

Here we go. The rumblings of a plan formed in Harrison's head. Maybe this was a bad idea. It might be the sort of one-sided decision that Nolan just berated him for, and he'd be totally right. But a grand gesture was required here, and a grand gesture was what Nolan deserved.

Because Harrison loved him, too.

Chapter 29

Nolan didn't hear from Harrison that day, nor the day after.

But life went on.

He was at the salon Wednesday morning when Roxanne from End of the Rainbow Rescues texted him. They had found and approved an adopter for Bandit and Smokey, and could Nolan please get them ready and drop them off later that evening? Heavy hands sent the reply. Yeah, he'd gotten attached to the dogs, and while having a real forever home was better than hanging out with two guys in an apartment, they'd be sorely missed.

Diego's car was in his parking spot when Nolan pulled up. "You here?" Nolan called out.

"In my room." Nolan leaned against the door frame and looked down at Diego, who sat on his bed and strummed his guitar for the puppies, who flopped inelegantly on the floor and listened to the music. "You're home early."

Nolan nodded. "The dogs got adopted. I'm supposed to get them ready and take them over to meet their new family tonight." Nolan glanced back at the clock on his phone; he only had a couple hours to gather their things. "Noah's picking us up. After we drop them off, we're grabbing dinner. You wanna come?"

Diego's face fell. "Aw shit. I mean, good for them, but I'm gonna miss the little bastards." As if on cue, Bandit scampered over toward Diego and leaned against his legs. "But I've got some good news too that we can celebrate. The lawsuit is over. They dropped their case."

Nolan's jaw dropped. "What?"

Diego set his guitar down and stroked Bandit. "Yeah. Mr. Crawford found some video on that day you guys went looking at the accident scene. He spotted an ATM camera and had been waiting for the bank to release the video to them. It shows that she never even hit her brakes when she slammed into us."

It was over.

"Congrats, man. I bet you're feeling good." Nolan reached over and clapped Diego on the shoulder. "And I'm sorry for all the shit I put you through, and any stress that I added to your situation this last month."

But Diego shook his head. "No, man, nothing to be sorry about. I just wish it had worked out for you guys. Haven't heard from him?"

Smokey dropped in front of them, and Nolan scratched his belly. He smiled, despite the sadness in his voice. "Nope. And maybe I won't. But I did all that I could do, and I'm not sure what I would do different. I wouldn't dance with Jake, but even that—all that showed me was that at some point, he'd have found some reason to end our relationship because of his insecurities."

Diego nodded. "That's real mature of you."

"Yeah," Nolan said with a smirk. "It happens sometimes."

Diego lifted Smokey to his face and kissed him. "You need any help to get them ready?" He sniffed the puppy's fur, his nose wrinkling at the puppy musk. "Maybe a quick bath?"

Nolan snickered. "Yeah, that sounds good. Thanks for your help."

Noah: *I'm here. Do you need help?*
Me: *Nope. On our way down.*

Nolan got into the backseat of Noah's Prius with the dogs. Diego slid into the passenger side. "Where are we dropping them off? What part of town?" Diego asked as Noah pulled out of the parking lot.

Nolan looked down at his phone and found the group chat with the information. "Roxanne said we're meeting the adopter at a McAllister Park. He wants to take them back to his house." Nolan shrugged. "I guess it's a surprise for the family."

Diego grinned. "That sounds fun. See guys, you've got a great life in store ahead of you." Noah lowered one of the windows in the backseat, and they poked their heads out, joyfully sniffing the air as they drove.

The park wasn't too far away, and the hurt started as Noah found a parking spot. It wasn't just saying goodbye to the dogs, though that was always hard. But saying goodbye to them symbolized the end of a lot of things, both good and bad. Diego's case was over, but so was Nolan's relationship with Harrison. He'd given Harrison his heart so easily—too easily, maybe, and that was a lesson to learn as well.

Nolan wasn't the same person he was back in January when Diego took him out to the club to shake him out of his funk. Older and wiser, and the next time Nolan gave someone his heart, he wouldn't be so scared about what they think of him.

Roxanne hadn't sent the adopter's information in the chat, which was odd, but Noah seemed to know what he was doing. "Roxanne texted me earlier. I know where we're going."

The three men walked around for a minute, and Nolan looked for someone who looked like they were waiting for their dogs. Laughter bubbled from a playground full of kids, and people jogged past them along a trail. After they walked the dogs toward a grassy patch near the dog park, Nolan paused. "I don't understand why they didn't give us a contact number."

Noah sighed loudly, and Diego grinned at him.

"What? What am I missing here?"

And then—Nolan saw him.

Harrison sat over on a blanket under a tree. When he saw Nolan, he stood and hesitantly held up a hand.

None of this made sense. Why was he here? The depositions were over, and they had dropped the lawsuit. Harrison didn't want to see Nolan anymore—right?

Nolan walked toward him with the dogs. "What are you doing here?" Realization washed over him. "Wait—you're the adopter?"

His slow smile was bright like the sun. "I am. You know better than anyone that I've got the room, and it's too lonely in that house for just me." Harrison bent down, and the puppies ran toward him, always excited to see new people. "What do you think?" he asked as he sat back down.

What did he think? Emotions blurred—his heartache for Harrison with the joy that the dogs would end up together in such a great place. "They're gonna love it at your house." He knelt on the blanket, still holding their leashes, and peering around at all the toys Harrison brought for them, rope bones and squeaky toys. Nolan picked up a rainbow bandana and wetness pricked at the corners of his eyes. "This is cute."

"I liked it." Harrison's eyes lit up as the puppies scrambled over him. "Nolan, I'm sorry I was such an ass. I was wrong to not talk to you about what happened, and I'd understand if you didn't want to speak with me anymore. But I miss you."

A terrible thought occurred to him. "Tell me you didn't adopt the dogs just to impress me, because pet ownership is a big—"

Nolan didn't get any further. Harrison leaned forward, tipped his head toward Nolan and they kissed, soft and perfect. When Nolan's eyes opened, everything was brighter, and his heart thumped in his chest again. "That's one way of shutting me up, I guess."

Harrison laughed, a deep rumble in his chest. "Oh, I missed you."

"Nolan!"

Crap, he'd forgotten about the others. Noah and Diego stood several yards away, giving them some privacy. They waved at Harrison and Noah gave Nolan a thumbs-up sign. When Nolan returned it, he smiled, and they turned and walked back toward the parking lot.

Nolan glanced at Harrison, and hope filled his heart. Could they start again, two people on even ground, both willing to take a chance on a relationship that some people might find unconventional? "You mind taking me home later?"

"I will, I promise. Whenever you're ready. But maybe—" Bandit ran back up between them, vying for Harrison's attention, and Nolan laughed. "Maybe you can come back to my place for a little while and help me get them settled. We could talk about us." His fingers stroked Nolan's hand. "I could apologize some more."

Joy bubbled up inside Nolan. "That sounds like a brilliant plan."

But as good as it felt, being back with Harrison, they still had a lot to talk through before that lingering awkwardness dissipated. Harrison reached for Nolan's hand in the car, but neither man spoke until they reached Harrison's house. "Welcome home, boys," Harrison said, as the garage door automatically opened, and he pulled his car inside.

Nolan followed Harrison into his house, and together they set up the dog crates in an extra downstairs room.

"This floor feels like foam," Nolan said and sat down on the floor, pressing his hand against it.

"This was my ex-wife's yoga room." Harrison snapped the baby gate into place on the door. "I thought that it might be nicer against their paws, but if they don't like it, I can rip it out, or give them another room."

"If they don't like it?" Nolan asked with a grin. "Are they going to complain about it?"

"Sounds silly, I guess." Harrison chuckled and sat down next to Nolan. "Eventually I'll get rid of that gate, once the house is completely safe for them. And it's only for when I'm not home. The rest of the time, they'll be with me, watching TV or hanging out in the backyard..."

Neither man spoke, both watching the dogs as they investigated the room, sniffing the corners and baskets of toys. "I guess we should talk about what happened," Nolan said slowly.

"Part of me wants to just pretend it never happened and pick up where we were." Harrison smiled as Smokey rambled toward him and flopped into his lap. He stroked the dog's belly with a finger. "But I don't guess that's the smart move."

Nolan shook his head. "Let's do this right, Harry. If this —" Nolan moved his finger between them—"if this thing between you and me is as important as I think it could be, we deserve it to each other to do it right, and that means being open and honest, especially when we hurt each other." Nolan reached for Harrison's hand. "I know I hurt you. Never ever in a million years did I want that to happen, but it did, and I have to take responsibility for it. I have to apologize and ask your forgiveness. And you have to hear me say that, and hopefully forgive me."

"It's okay—" Harrison began, but Nolan stopped him.

"No, it was not okay." Nolan didn't let go of Harrison's hand as he spoke, that touch grounding him. "I was upset and mad at you that night. These wild thoughts were running through my head, that you didn't want to be seen with me, and that you didn't care about my feelings. But I didn't want Jake. Never at any point in that night did I want him to touch me— but I let it happen, and I apologize for that. It will never happen again." Nolan's voice waivered at those last words. "I promise you that."

Harrison moved closer to Nolan and kissed his cheek. "I accept your apology." He cleared his throat. "I guess it's my turn, right?" But Harrison didn't speak right away. He pressed his fingertips against Nolan's and laced their hands together. "You scared me, Nolan."

"How?"

"I was okay with nothing and had made peace with being alone. But then you dangled happiness in front of me. This beautiful boy, funny and handsome and sexy and—" Harrison stopped and took a breath. "You breathed life into me and then I was afraid of what it would feel like, losing you. You're so damn young," he said, pushing a loose strand of hair behind Nolan's ear. "Your whole life is ahead of you, and it didn't seem fair to you, being with me." He snickered, but it was a low, bitter sound. "So, I pushed you away before you got the chance to really hurt me. Everything you said was right. I acted like being older meant I knew more than you, when all you have ever done, since that first day we met, is teach me what it means to be a man. I am so, so sorry I ignored your feelings and disregarded your input in what our relationship should be." Another smile, this one more hopeful, tugged at his lips. "I apologize for that, and it will never happen again."

Now it was Nolan's turn to lean in and kiss Harrison's cheek. "Better not." The dogs lay next to them, curled up together in their sleep. "Let's show these guys their new backyard, eh? Can't wait to see them running around." Nolan stood, and held his hands out to Harrison, helping him up. "Are you going to let them sleep with you?"

Harrison's arm wrapped around Nolan's as they lifted the baby gate and walked out of the room, the puppies excitedly scampering behind them. "I'm sure they'll spend many nights upstairs with me." He stopped just as they got to the door leading to the backyard and leaned in for a soft kiss. "But probably not tonight."

Nolan closed his eyes at that sweet kiss, unable to keep the smile off his face as it ended. "No, definitely not tonight."

The ceiling fan in Harrison's bedroom spun slowly over their tangled bodies as moonlight illuminated Harrison's bedroom. Nolan arched his back as Harrison slowly mouthed over his chest, his tongue teasing Nolan's hard nipples, and tracing a slow path down his torso.

Harrison was on a mission to kiss and lick and nibble every inch of Nolan's body.

All of this was still so new for them, being together like this, learning each other's bodies—and Nolan hoped it would always be this way, and they'd never grow tired of these tender explorations. He groaned as heat and pleasure rushed through him, and when Harrison's fingers pressed against his wrinkled hole, his breath hitched, and his legs spread wide, and one knee hooked over Harrison's shoulder.

Nolan shivered at the intrusion, and his hand gently threaded through Harrison's soft hair, then tightened in those dark tresses lined with silver that had delighted him when they first met.

When Harrison slid deep in Nolan's tight passage, fuck, that sweet stretch felt so good, and Harrison paused, braced up on his elbows and fully seated inside Nolan. He let out a shaky breath. "Love you," he rasped against Nolan's lips.

Nolan answered with a biting kiss and wrapped his legs around Harrison's hips. "Show me," he whispered, and groaned at each deep thrust that punched the breath out of him. Over and over, Harrison drove into his body, dropping kisses all along Nolan's jaw and throat and when he came, it was like a roar in Nolan's ear.

Nolan fell back into the bed, feeling more than a little victorious seeing his strong, quiet man come apart. He reached for Harrison's hand as they lay together, their legs tangled, and Harrison's head on his chest. "I missed you."

"Me too." Harrison looked up and caught Nolan's eyes. "You've got so much to teach me," he said, and dropped kisses all along Nolan's chest.

That made Nolan smile, imagining everything they could teach each other, both in and out of this amazing bed. "Could take years," he said, and tipped his head down for a kiss.

Could take a lifetime.

Chapter 30

*T*wo months later

...and while I'm sad to be leaving the firm and all the friends I've made during my seventeen years here, I know that this change is the beginning of a new chapter in my life.

Hitting SEND on that email hurt more than Harrison expected, but it was the right decision. Jenny had been wrong—Harrison's business partners didn't reject him, personally or professionally, when they learned about his sexual orientation. But it was time to make a change, and this time seemed as good as any. He'd worked at this firm for a good chunk of his adult life and was grateful for every minute. But if he didn't try something new, he'd stagnate in this room for another decade until it was all over, and there was so much Harrison had yet to accomplish.

But it still hurt. Several boxes were stacked in the center of the room, filled with personal items and his legal books, all waiting to be picked up by Troy and Diego and taken back to his house. Harrison's home office, which had never seen much use, was now the headquarters for his new law practice while he arranged to lease some office space in a new building.

The last months spent getting to know and understand the LGBT community and their unique legal issues led Harrison to the decision to leave his firm and start his own legal practice where he could try to make a difference in their community.

In *his* community.

Alicia walked into the office and shook her head at all the boxes and empty walls. She blinked quickly and touched the corner of her eye. "It won't be the same here without you, sir."

The lump in Harrison's throat made him pause before speaking. "Thanks for saying that. Between you and me, I'm more than a little scared to be starting something new. But it feels good too, that excitement."

Alicia nodded. "The end of an era. But starting that new business—*your new business*—it's going to feel so good." She chuckled and wiped away a tear. "And when the time comes and you need an office manager or personal assistant, I had better be your first call."

They hugged. "Absolutely. But I know that Ms. Chin is going to rely on your knowledge and expertise during her first few months in this office." It had delighted Harrison when the partners decided that in addition to hiring two new lawyers to help with their caseload, they'd offered his office to Jania Chin. "I have a feeling that before too long, the two of you will be running this place."

She lowered her voice. "I said the same thing to Rocco just this morning."

A knock at the door caught their attention. Ben Barton stood in the doorway and glanced around. "So, it's really happening."

"Afraid so, Ben," Harrison answered.

Alicia gave him a quick wink and then left the room as Ben walked in. "I don't have to tell you that you'll be missed here, but I'm proud as hell of what you're doing. You'll do good work, and I think it'll be fulfilling, on a personal level." He snorted, leaning against Harrison's desk. "On a professional level, it's a great idea too. The next decade or two is going to be filled with legal precedents and challenges. Objectively speaking, it's a brilliant business decision."

"That's not why I'm doing this," Harrison said, and then laughed. "But you're not wrong. There's a lot of legislation out there that needs fixing." Could Harrison help protect the rights of his friends and community in his city and in his state?

He hoped so.

The front entryway to the house filled with boxes as Harrison unpacked and decided what could stay packed. The sound of laughter rang in the hallway, so he peeked around the corner and spotted Diego on the floor of the living room, Smokey and Bandit climbing him like their own personal playground. "They missed you."

"I missed them too."

Troy joined them in the living room and grinned when the dogs scampered toward him.

"Hey Dad, would it be okay if we hung out here a while, maybe went swimming?"

Harrison beamed. "Of course, you are always welcome here. And the dogs love to swim too. Take them in the pool with you."

Troy and Diego talked excitedly about their plans for the weekend as they headed outside, the dogs following them.

If Harrison had known that getting a dog would have brought his son around more often, he'd have done it a long time ago.

After an hour of unpacking, Harrison joined them outside and sat on the patio while they played in the water. He took a couple of pictures and sent them to Nolan.

Nolan: *I'm the only one toiling away at work on this beautiful afternoon.*

Harrison: *It appears so.*
Nolan: *I miss your face. We still on for tomorrow night?*
Harrison: *Yes. Can't wait to see you. Love you.*
Nolan: *Love you too*
"Hey Dad!"
Harrison looked up. "Yeah?"
Troy sat on the side of the pool, watching as Diego tossed tennis balls into the water and the dogs leapt in after them. "Do you think we can use your dogs in a music video? Trevor wants us to work on increasing our following beyond the Montrose area. D and I were just talking about maybe filming something here with the two of them swimming around and inter-cut with us playing our instruments."

"That's a great idea," Harrison answered, and laughed at the picture in his head.

"Mr. Crawford?" Despite many attempts to persuade him otherwise, Diego was incapable of calling him by his first name; Harrison understood. "Did Nolan tell you about my birthday barbeque at his mom's house next weekend?"

"He did, and I promised we'd be there." A few butterflies still fluttered around in Harrison's stomach at the idea of spending time with Nolan's family, holding his hand in front of his mother, who had so far seemed supportive. But Harrison understood her apprehension, and only wanted to show her, and their friends, how much he loved and cherished her amazing son.

Troy reached for a ball and tossed it into the water, and they laughed as Smokey, laser focused, dove in after it. "My birthday's in July. We should get everyone together here and have a pool party." He looked up. "If that's okay with you, Dad."

If that was okay with me...

Harrison's big empty house didn't seem quite as lonely as it used to be, and maybe by July, it wouldn't be, if he had his way. "I think that's a fabulous idea."

Chapter 31

"Higher on the left. Higher. Okay, right there. Wait—"

Nolan turned and narrowed his eyes. "Why don't you come up here and do this?" He stood perched on top of a small stepladder, apparently incapable of hanging the Happy Birthday banner to Noah's exacting standards.

But Noah shook his head. "You've almost got it. Just—okay, like that. Don't move it." Nolan taped the banner up and stepped off the ladder, growling at him. "You're always such a dramatic queen," Noah said, and took the tape from Nolan's hands.

"You're not wrong, but that's not the point. Why are you always such a grouchy gay? For real, this is supposed to be a party." But Noah's eyes darkened, and his shoulders slumped. Uh-oh.

Nolan bumped his shoulder. "Something wrong?"

Noah snorted. "It's nothing. Just—" He looked around the yard. "I don't think we'll be seeing Martin here today."

Nolan frowned. "Aw man. I'm sorry."

"No, don't worry about it. I knew it wasn't going to be forever, but, fuck, man, I hate being lied to... you know?"

"Yeah."

Noah took a deep breath, and shook his head, like he wanted to will himself into a better mood. "Fuck that guy.

We're having a party today, right?"

"Hell yeah." It was on the tip of Nolan's tongue to say something about Noah being a great guy, and how he'd find someone of his own one day, but today wasn't the day for that. Not with him and his own boyfriend radiating their own happiness, bright as the sun.

But maybe some other news Nolan had would please his brother. "So—I talked to the advisor over at San Jacinto College, and she helped me register for classes." Excitement bubbled up inside him as he talked about this dream, finally able to share it with his family. "I'm gonna start this summer, just a couple of classes to get my feet wet again."

That did it. Noah's eyes brightened, and he pulled Nolan into a tight hug. "That makes me so happy, little brother," he said, and even though Nolan hated that nickname, he hugged back as tight as he could. "What's the game plan? And can I help you with anything?"

"First, the advisor's looking at what credits I have completed that will transfer over, and we can see what I'd need to take to get an associate's degree in business management. Once I'm done with that, if I want to go to a bigger university I can transfer it all over." Nolan bit his lip and wrinkled his nose. "But just getting the two-year degree might be enough to help get me started on opening my own salon one day."

"Definitely." The brothers headed inside, where people had begun to gather in the kitchen. Bowls of chips and snacks lined the countertop, and Nolan grabbed a handful of popcorn. "You've got a lot of real-world experience too, and in some ways that's just as important."

Noah's genuine enthusiasm shone on his face, and Nolan's heart twisted inside. Why had he waited so long to share this dream with his family? "As to your second question," Nolan began, then stopped. Harrison had just arrived. He held a gift bag, and his eyes darted the room, searching Nolan out. Nolan grinned at the way Harrison's eyes brightened when he found him and waved him over. "I know I'll probably need help with papers and stuff. I'm not the best writer and can't spell for shit."

Harrison set the bag down on the gift table and slipped his arm around Nolan. "Hey handsome," Nolan said and kissed his cheek.

"Hi you. Hello Noah," Harrison said, and nodded at his brother. "Good to see you." His eyes darted around. "Where's the birthday boy?"

"On his way." Nolan pulled his phone out of his pocket and peered at the latest message. "His sister says they're about fifteen minutes out." Harrison's arm dropped to his side, and he straightened. Noah's lips quirked into a grin. *What was going on?* Nolan looked around.

Oh. Their mother had made her way over toward them. "Mom, you remember Harrison, right?" Nolan asked. Dani had wanted to meet Harrison officially as soon as Nolan told her they were back together, so they took her out for dinner at a fancy restaurant. The age thing was awkward, and that couldn't be helped, but Harrison had some great stories about the dogs that seemed to ease her mind about what kind of man he was.

That, and the way Harrison treated him. Maybe it sounded silly to some people, but Nolan had never felt treasured like this before.

Harrison pulled out his phone and showed them the most recent pictures of the dogs. Dani couldn't get over how they jumped into the pool and swam around after their toys. "Those are some incredibly lucky dogs," she said.

"I feel like the lucky one." Harrison's arm snaked around Nolan again, and he leaned into him. "Between Nolan and the boys, it's like I've rediscovered my life again."

Yeah, Nolan blushed. They'd make fun of him later, but he didn't care.

The previous night, they'd gone walking around Buffalo Bayou after having dinner with some of Harrison's friends,

Donna Keller and her husband Bart. As they walked around, they heard music playing and discovered a jazz concert going on. They stood and listened for a few minutes, and Harrison reached for his hand like it was the most natural thing in the world. Yeah, a couple of people stared, but Nolan didn't even think Harrison noticed—or cared.

So much had changed in the last couple of months. Nolan went from being cheated on to cherished by this loving man, and for the first time in his life, he knew exactly where he was headed, surrounded by love and support of friends, family, and his Harry.

And it was only going to get better.

About Argentina

Argentina Ryder spent her early career as a high school teacher in Texas, sharing her love of geography and traveling with her students. After completing her masters in education, she worked as a curriculum and instruction consultant while working on her first novel.

Argentina's bucket list includes visiting all the national parks and running a ten-minute mile. She spends free time in her garden, kayaking Texas rivers, and littering her house with various DIY projects. Her red slider, Pebbles, enjoys frozen strawberries, basking under her UV light, and spending quality time outside on sunny days while Lucrezia, her Siamese, mostly just sleeps.

She lives with her family and her pets and is currently working on the next books in her Paws and Claws and Rio Riendo series. Sign up for her newsletter at argentinaryder.com to keep up with what's going on in her world and get sneak peeks at what's coming up.